D1010691

It's Girls Like You, Mickey

It's Girls Like You, Mickey

Patti Kim

Atheneum Books for Young Readers
NEW YORK LONDON TORONTO SYDNEY NEW DELHI

Acknowledgments

It's because of my editor Reka Simonsen that I am on friendly terms with rewriting. She has transformed for me what used to be a task of torture into a journey of intriguing possibilities and downright fun. My heartfelt gratitude to Michelle Humphrey, Justin Chanda, Julia McCarthy, Sarah Woodruff, Jeannie Ng, Genevieve Santos, and Lisa Moraleda.

ATHENEUM BOOKS FOR YOUNG READERS • An imprint of Simon & Schuster Children's Publishing Division • 1230 Avenue of the Americas, New York, New York 10020 • This book is a work of fiction. Any references to historical events, real people, or real places are used fictitiously. Other names, characters, places, and events are products of the author's imagination, and any resemblance to actual events or places or persons, living or dead, is entirely coincidental. • Text copyright © 2020 by Patti Kim • Jacket illustration copyright © 2020 by Genevieve Santos • All rights reserved, including the right of reproduction in whole or in part in any form. • ATHENEUM BOOKS FOR YOUNG READERS is a registered trademark of Simon & Schuster, Inc. Atheneum logo is a trademark of Simon & Schuster, Inc. • For information about special discounts for bulk purchases, please contact Simon & Schuster Special Sales at 1-866-506-1949 or business@simonandschuster.com. • The Simon & Schuster Speakers Bureau can bring authors to your live event. For more information or to book an event, contact the Simon & Schuster Speakers Bureau at 1-866-248-3049 or visit our website at www.simonspeakers.com. • The text for this book was set in New Century Schoolbook LT. • Manufactured in the United States of America • 0520 BVG • First Edition • 10 9 8 7 6 5 4 3 2 1 • Library of Congress Cataloging-in-Publication Data • Names: Kim, Patti, 1970– author. • Title: It's girls like you, Mickey / Patti Kim. • Other titles: It is girls like you, Mickey • Description: First edition. | New York : Atheneum Books for Young Readers, 2020. | Audience: Ages 10 up. | Audience: Grades 4–6. | Summary: Mickey faces a lot of challenges when starting seventh grade, but an instant connection with new student Sun Joo improves her outlook until Sydney, popular and mean, decides to make Sun Joo her friend. • Identifiers: LCCN 2019043789 | ISBN 9781534443457 (hardcover) | ISBN 9781534443471 (eBook) • Subjects: CYAC: Friendship—Fiction. | Popularity—Fiction. | Middle schools—Fiction. | Schools—Fiction. | Korean Americans—Fiction. | Poverty—Fiction. | Single-parent families—Fiction. • Classification: LCC PZ7.1.K5835 It 2020 | DDC [Fic]—dc23 • LC record available at https://lccn.loc.gov/2019043789

*To Sophie, Ellie,
and John,
for loving me
silly and steady*

one

It ain't normal for me to feel nervous about nothing, but I got knots this morning. It's the first day of seventh grade. I'm feeling shy. I'm a lot of things, but shy's not one of them, so I don't know what's wrong with me.

I went through, like, umpteen million outfits before I settled on this one. A pair of old pink tights I turned into leggings by cutting open the feet 'cause they're too short for me. My daddy's faded old T-shirt with KEEP ON TRUCKIN' across the front. It was one of his favorites, but he left it behind. Finders keepers. Losers weepers. I hope he's weeping, 'cause I'm done with weeping. I belted the shirt with twine I braided. Dangling off the two ends are clusters of paper clips in rainbow colors.

Didn't get to go back-to-school shopping. After we got home from Ocean City, my ma was sore in ways I can't even start to describe, and that made her good and fed up with Benny and me. Daddy didn't come back home with us. I should've held my tongue, but I brought up how we needed school supplies and new shoes and clothes, especially Benny 'cause he'd get plastered showing up first day of third grade in my old flip-flops. Ma lost it. She lit a cigarette, inhaled big like she was fueling up to smoke me alive, evil-eyed me, crossed her legs, and shook her foot like it was revving up to kick me across the living room.

Then our yellow Lab, Charlie, sat next to her on the couch. Ma rested her hand on his head and said, "Well, then, I guess Charlie's gotta go."

"No, Ma," I said.

"Dog food don't grow on trees. Up to y'all," she said.

"I got an idea. You could quit them cigarettes," I said.

Benny started whimpering and hugging all over Charlie, and I could feel my heart cracking into a million pieces.

"In your dreams, Mick. You could quit eating," she said, and blew out a long stream of smoke.

"Ma, I need food to stay alive. You don't need no cigarettes to stay alive. You telling me you'd rather have your daughter starve to death so you can keep smoking them cancer sticks?"

I was going to slap her with "What kind of mother are you?" but I held back. Her foot was twitching so mad that her slipper flung off. And she wasn't bothering with no ashtray. Her trigger-happy thumb flicked ash everywhere, burning tiny black holes on the carpet and the couch. She didn't snap back at me like she normally does with some whip sting of a comeback. She just fidgeted all nervous, looking like she was at a loss. Then her lips trembled like she was about to cry.

Ma raised me and Benny by three rules: Don't cry. Don't beg. Chin up.

Ma is country strong. Daddy used to say she's built Ford tough. She grew up on a farm in Ohio, tending to horses, cows, chickens, and pigs. She killed chickens with her bare hands. She got no mind for fairy tales and beauty pageants and princess tears. She hated me being in all them pageants. Didn't make no bit of sense to her.

When I saw Ma's eyes filling with tears, I knew we were in a bad way. A weight of worry came knocking at my gut. I felt sorry, so I folded and said, "Never mind. We'll make do."

So this here outfit's how I'm making do. At least I'm having a good hair day. I fashioned myself a nice thick headband using Daddy's one and only necktie, teased the top of my hair poofy and flipped up the ends so I look like Frances "Gidget" Lawrence. Yeah, Gidget from that old TV show nobody but me watches. I'm not one to get easily roped in by sap and circumstance, but that girl makes me happy. That last snapshot in the intro of her being kissed on the cheek by Don Porter, who plays her dad, always makes me sigh.

I sigh, checking myself out one last time in the mirror.

Stuck on the frame of the mirror is my friend Ok's postcard. I miss him. He was my one and only buddy at school last year. I kind of forced him to be my friend, but there weren't no way we would've ended up friends if I hadn't. I taught him how to roller-skate. We did the talent show together. He braided my hair. A whole big thing went down with him running away from home, which ended up happily ever after, thanks to yours truly, you're welcome. I practically saved his life. I wish he hadn't moved.

First day of seventh grade would be a slice of key lime pie if I knew Ok was going to be on that bus saving me a seat. Or in that cafeteria eating his Korean food, waiting for me to sit next to him.

Instead, I'm going to be all by my lonesome again. Worst thing about not having a friend is there ain't no Teflon. There ain't no home base. There ain't no one to stand next to and feel like weirdos together. By myself, I'm an open target. It don't help none that I'm so proud. It's the pride that brings on the attacks. They see me like I'm some poor fat lazy white trailer trash who shouldn't dare express herself, let alone be proud. Who does she think she is?

I wish I didn't care about the teasing, but I do. I put on a good show and act like it don't bother me none, but it does.

Where's Ok Lee when I need him? He's way in another county, that's where. I'll bet he's a bundle of nerves too, 'cause he's starting a brand-new school. And I know for a fact he did not grow one inch over the summer or don't look any less Chinese. That's how they teased him, no matter how many times I told them he ain't Chinese—he's Korean. Fat poor white girl and skinny little Chinese boy with porcupine hair. Together, we were a team of Teflon.

I miss him. We're pen pals now. He sent me a postcard cut out of a Life cereal box. L-I-F-E in rainbow colors. "Who's there?" was written on the back. The only reason he did that was 'cause I sent him a postcard I cut out from a mac and cheese box with "Knock! Knock!" written on the back. I guess it's my turn now to answer who's doing the knocking.

"Michaela Shannon McDonald," I say to my reflection with my back straight and fists on hips. "Get out there and be your absolute ultimate."

two

The science teacher looks like Tinker Bell. She's the size of a fairy. On the top of her head sits a bun that reminds me of a Pillsbury Grands! Homestyle buttermilk biscuit. She walks like she's gliding onto a stage. I'll bet she was a ballerina back in the day.

She writes her name on the board. TRZETRZE-LEWSKA. She pronounces it. Her voice don't match her looks. She sounds like she chain-smokes five packs a day. And when she says her name, it's like a train with a lisp chugging along some tracks badly needing repairs. She didn't even bother teaching us how to say it. She told us just to call her Ms. T and said, "I pity the fool."

Some of us groan. Some chuckle.

We get assigned seats. Two to a table. In alphabetical order. Lab partners for the entire year. The kids whine, but I don't mind it. I think assigned seating's a good idea. It keeps a kid from being the odd one out. I'll bet if we had assigned seating during lunch, it'd save a bunch of kids from being nervous wrecks.

Ms. T goes down the list like she's deaf to the fussing. She comes to the *M*s.

"Michaela McDonald," she calls.

"It's Mickey, please," I say.

"Mickey."

I take a seat.

"Sun Joo Moon," Ms. T calls.

No answer.

"Sun Joo Moon?" she calls out again.

No one steps forward.

Great. Just great. Ain't I the lucky duck, getting stuck with a real winner like this Sun Joo Moon kid. Can't even tell if it's a boy or a girl. What I can gather is that Sun Joo Moon can't show up on the first day of school. What loser skips out on the first day of school? I'll tell you. A lifelong ne'er-do-well, a certified good-for-nothing.

So while everyone else gets a partner, I'm stuck here with an empty chair. *Hi. How'd your summer go? Mine was the pits. Lost a friend and my daddy all in one fun-in-the-sun sweep.*

Ain't no reason for me to take it personal, but it feels personal. It's the first day of sixth grade all over again. Ain't middle school supposed to get easier? I'm getting all knotted up thinking about walking into that cafeteria, and lunch don't happen for three hours.

Every table's got two textbooks. One for me. One for my missing partner. *Life Science*. The cover's got a picture of a shark. Some budding artist from years past drew a stickman clamped between the shark's teeth. Fat drip-drops of blood. The fattest drip-drop's got HELP written in it.

The tabletop is black and sticky and all scarred up with cuts and gashes. I don't know if this rumor's true, but I heard seventh graders had to dissect pickled worms, frogs, rats, cats, and piglets. I try not to think about it, but the more I hear Ms. T's gravel-hard voice, the more I'm convinced she might be into that kind of thing. Suddenly, the air smells like nail polish remover, and my head feels like it's stuffed with feathers.

Ms. T gets down to business. She erases her long name and writes "CELL" on the board. No icebreaker. No getting-to-know-you games. She tells us to open our textbooks to a diagram of a plant cell. Looks just like a cartoon. Heavy on the bright colors. Mega eager beaver to be liked. Desperate for attention. Screaming all-eyes-on-me. The big blue glob is called a vacuole. Pink, blue, green, red, and purple critters surround it. Reminds me of a lava lamp. Makes me sleepy just looking at it.

I yawn.

Then suddenly I'm wide-awake, 'cause standing at

the door is our guidance counselor, Mr. Fox, with a new family. They look like Koreans. I guess they could be Chinese or Japanese or Vietnamese or any number of Asianese, but I'd put my money on Koreans on account of my friend Ok Lee being Korean and that's just what I'm used to and I guess that's just what I'm sorta wishing for since him and me got along so good and I'm missing my friend.

"Good morning, Ms. T," Mr. Fox says, tapping the door with his knuckles. His mustache looks like a hairy horseshoe hanging out of his nostrils.

She looks up over her glasses, which are about to slide off the tip of her nose.

"I apologize for interrupting. We have a new family. This is Mr. and Mrs. Moon. This is their daughter, Sun. Did I get that right? Or is it Sun Joo? What would you prefer to be called?" Mr. Fox asks.

The girl don't answer. She's hanging her head so low, from where I'm sitting, she could pass for being headless. She leans against her mother, who nudges her away and whispers something to her. I'll bet it's *aigo-aigo*, which is what Ok's mom used to say when she got fed up. It sounds just like "I go, I go," which makes bingo sense 'cause it's like saying "I'm sicka this. I'm done. I'm outta here." I go. I go.

The girl's fear is filling up the room like Benny's

9

farts fill up our apartment after he eats pork 'n' beans.

I got a mix of sweet and sour feelings about this girl. On the one hand, I feel sorry for her like I want to pop out of my seat, take her by the wrist, lead her to the chair next to mine, and tell her everything's going to be all right. On the other hand, I feel frustrated like I want to take her by the shoulders and give her a good shaking and a strong talking-to about how this is her one and only life and there ain't no time to waste on being scared and feeling like you're less than. Chin up.

"Moon, Sun Joo," the dad says.

"Moon?" Mr. Fox asks.

"Yes," the dad says.

"All right. This is Moon," Mr. Fox says.

"Your seat's right there," Ms. T says, pointing her nose to my table.

I raise my hand.

Some kid in the back fake-coughs to cover up calling her a Moonie.

Some other kid chuckles.

I raise my arm and wave my hand 'cause I got something to say.

"Yes?" Ms. T says.

"Yes, ma'am. Mickey here. I just want to clarify that the new student's last name is Moon. That's just how they order names in their country. The last name comes first.

The first name comes second, and the middle name comes last. So I'm pretty sure she don't want to be called Moon, Mr. Fox, just like you don't want to be called Fox," I say.

The class laughs.

"Is that right?" Mr. Fox asks the dad.

"Yes," he says, and nods.

"Her name Sun Joo," the mom says, and nudges the girl into the classroom.

Her body moves like a puppet on strings. She don't want to come in. I can actually make out the top of her backpack 'cause her chin is digging a hole in her chest.

Mr. Fox, her mom, and her dad leave, shutting the door behind them. This here's where Sun Joo's gotta decide if she's going to be a baby and go chasing after her mommy and daddy or if she's going to girl up and claim her rightful seat or if she's going to just stand there like a zombie.

One one thousand. Two one thousand. Three one thousand. Four one thousand. I'm counting in my head. I'm at six one thou- when she hustles over to our table and sits down. Just like that. In a blink. She moved lightning quick. Ants-in-her-pants quick. Like she was thinking the faster, the better. Like when you gotta peel off a Band-Aid? You don't wanna take your time with pain. You wanna get that over with.

I wanna give her a high five, but the poor thing is

frozen stiff again. Can't even take off her backpack. Head's hanging down. Back's curled like a roly-poly. I wonder if a poke will straighten her up.

Ms. T's going on and on about the mighty mitochondria, how nothing can do nothing without it 'cause it's the engine that makes energy out of food. Food. Lunch. Cafeteria. I get to worrying again, not so much for me, but for my new lab partner. If she thinks making this entrance was hard, wait till lunch. Her head's going to be hanging so low, she'll be sweeping the floor with her bangs.

three

I'm inching my way over to the cafeteria 'cause if I time it just so, I could end up spending most of lunch waiting in line for my food instead of wandering from table to table, wishing someone would take pity on me and let me sit next to them.

I'm not even thirsty, but I stop at the fountain and let the water wash over my lips.

I don't even need to go, but I stop at the bathroom, take a stall, count to thirty-seven, flush, wash my hands real thorough, dry them real thorough, and take a good hard look at myself in the mirror.

I give myself a strong talking to inside my head: Mickey McDonald, if you can't muster it up for yourself, then muster it up for that new girl, Sun Joo. Poor thing's probably lost in that cafeteria, don't know where to stand in line, don't know what she's eating, wandering from here to there, bumping into tables, getting called a Moonie. Poor thing needs you. Now go be your absolute ultimate.

I march out of the bathroom. I make my way to the cafeteria, dodging the eighth graders who roll through the hall like bowling balls. The doors are wide open like the mouth of some beast swallowing up kids and then spitting them out. The noise sounds like one ongoing burp.

I walk in. I stand in the free-lunch line. I don't know why they make the poor kids stand in a different line. Grilled cheese and tomato soup on the menu. I'm suddenly starving. I take a tray. I help myself to a carton of chocolate milk. It's sweating with condensation. I look around. I don't see her.

I do see Asa Banks. He's with his disciples. They always look like they're having such a time. Half of me says to get in there. Join in the fun. You're friends now 'cause of that thing that happened with Ok last year. Kinda-sorta. Other half says that's not where I belong, no matter what we went through. That was last year. This is now. One-on-one is one thing. Big setting like this is a whole other thing. Besides, I ain't all over the names he called me last year, and I want me my own disciples.

I'm so hungry I feel dizzy. I can't wait to sit down, so I take a big bite of my grilled cheese, the fat dripping down the corners of my lips. It's so greasy they oughta call it grease cheese. The tomato soup looks like what you'd throw up after eating tomato soup.

I don't see her.

There's Lawrence Elwood. He hugged me after the talent show last year. He said into my ear, "You should've won." He's sitting with Justin Hill, Shaundra Nelson, and Stacy Blake. Looks like a double date. Maybe I should've worn my roller skates today.

I still don't see her.

There's Sydney Stevenson. She's like the shining star of Landover Hills. She sits between her disciples, Nawsia Daniels and Tammy Radison. All three are wearing matching step team outfits—black leggings and red T-shirts that say HEAD OVER HILLS. Step's way cooler than cheerleading. If you make the HOH team, you got yourself a squad of automatic friends. I got a mind to ask about tryouts. I walk over and say, "Hi."

They don't hear me.

"Hi," I say louder.

I know they heard that, but they're ignoring me.

Getting ignored feels worse than getting teased. At least you're getting attention when you're being teased. This here's like you don't exist. I keep walking.

I still don't see her.

I need another bite of that grease cheese. I plop my tray down wherever, sit wherever, and wolf down my sandwich and gulp down the tomato soup, not bothering with a spork. As I'm washing it all down with chocolate milk, some kid nearby says, "Slow down, hungry, hungry hippo."

I look over. It's Frankie Doo-Doo. His last name's really Dooley, but he's famous for acting like a piece of doo-doo. He got the biggest, curliest ears that stick so far out they look like brain parts spilling out of the sides of his head. I should ignore him, but Landover Hills ain't no place for turning the other cheek, so I let my words shoot: "Hey, Mr. Potato Head, Dumbo wants his ears back."

The boys sitting nearby say, "Oooooooh." They laugh, punching one another's arms.

I catwalk over to the trash, take my chocolate pudding cup off my tray, and dump the rest of my lunch. There's an unopened pudding just sitting there in the bin, so I quickly grab that and strut out of the cafeteria, feeling sorry for insulting Dumbo 'cause I love Dumbo, and Frankie Doo-Doo ain't good enough to be likened to Dumbo, who's taught me to love what's different about me and use whatever holds me down to lift me up.

I stash my two pudding cups in my backpack and walk down the hall like I got a pair of wings. Like I just won the Little Miss Tiara pageant and I'm doing my victory lap. The noise coming out of the cafeteria? That's wild applause.

Twenty minutes to kill. I got nowhere to go. I stop

16

at the bulletin board where signup sheets are posted for organizing the winter dance, joining the Spanish club, trying out for cheerleading, and SGA nominations. I go through the list of nominations, looking for my name 'cause you never know. Someone might could've nominated me. Hope don't ever run dry in my heart. Looks like Nawsia and Tammy nominated Sydney Stevenson to run for president. Looks like Cookie Monster nominated Tinkie Winkie. My name's not on the list. If I had a friend who nominated me, oh boy oh boy, that'd be like winning the Powerball jackpot of friends.

I walk to the end of the hall. I grab the railing and go up the stairs like it's my mountain to climb. I'm fording streams. I'm following my rainbow. Then I hear whimpering. It sounds like Sabrina when she ain't feeling good. Sabrina's my oldest cat. I got three cats and a dog. Sabrina's got a long list of health problems. It makes me crazy sad to hear Ma say that kind of misery needs putting out.

I stop and bend down to look between the steps. There in the corner under the staircase sits a balled-up pill bug. I know the top of that head.

"There you are!" I call out through the steps.

I hurry down the stairs, plop myself down next to her, and say, "I've been looking for you. My name's Mickey. I'm your science partner. Remember?"

The girl's pressing her face into her kneecaps. Her arms are tight around her legs. Her sneakers are brand-spanking-new, whiter than fresh marshmallows. A rainbow, embroidered on the side, ends with BEST FRIEND in gold letters. Her double-knotted laces look plump like noodles, and instead of crisscross, she got them strung all lined up like a white picket fence. I'm shocked I didn't notice her shoes during science class 'cause they scream, *Look at me*.

"I like your sneakers," I say.

She's quiet. At least she don't sound like a sick cat no more.

I open my backpack, pull out two chocolate puddings, and ask, "Want one?"

No answer, but she does turn her head a little, peeking through her hair, which is acting like one of them bead curtains.

I'm trying to remember how to say hi in Korean. Ok taught me, but I can't remember it exact. Something like *onion-hi-say-yo-yo*?

"Here," I say, and hold up a pudding cup. "Go on. Take it. Bell's about to ring. Food ain't allowed in the classrooms, so eat up. It's good stuff."

I tap the cup against her fingers, but she don't take it.

"Fine," I say, and put it upside down on the top of her head.

I peel off my lid and take a lick of the pudding. Sun Joo's watching me, wearing that cup on her head like a mini top hat.

I dip two fingers into the pudding, scoop out a blob, smear a horseshoe mustache on my face, and do my best Mr. Fox, saying, "What's your name? Is it Moon? Is it Sun? Is it Joo?"

Pudding's dripping off my chin. She cracks a smile. I see her teeth through her curtain of hair. The cup on her head slides off, and like a pro, she catches it in her hand.

"Good catch," I say, and lick off some of the mustache. I wipe the rest with my daddy's tie.

She's holding her head up. With her chin pressed on her knees, she checks out the pudding cup. She peels back the lid nice and slow, sniffs it, takes a lick, and says, "Chocolate."

"Yeah, it's chocolate pudding," I say, and squeeze my cup so a blob rises to the top. I slurp it up.

She hands me the cup.

"You don't want it?" I ask.

"No, thank you," she says.

The way she's talking so polite and proper to me makes me feel like a grown-up.

"That's fine. More for me," I say, and take the cup. I squeeze it too hard, and the blob of pudding plop-lands on my leg, making a doo-doo stain on my pink tights.

"Oh no," Sun Joo says.

"*Aigo*," I say.

"You go?"

"Oh, I ain't going nowhere. I said *aigo*. It's Korean. Ain't you Korean? *Aigo, aigo*. Don't you say that when something don't go right?"

"Uhhhh. *Aigo*," she says, lifting her head up. First time I've seen her face without her hair acting like blinders.

Covering her mouth, Sun Joo nods and chuckles. I got her to laugh. She ain't balled up like a pill bug no more either. I lick the pudding off my leg. It's good stuff.

The bell rings.

four

I got me a lunch partner. Didn't take but three days for Sun Joo and me to come to an understanding that we should sit together in the cafeteria. I can't say we're best friends yet, but this here's the start of something, and it sure beats her crying under the stairs or me eating all by my lonesome and roaming the halls. We are, no doubt about it, the oddest of the oddballs of seventh grade, but who cares. We got each other for these thirty minutes. That's what counts.

Sun Joo waits for me at the back table. She don't take out her lunch box until I sit down with my tray of school lunch. I thought this was 'cause she was being all polite, but then I figured out it was 'cause she was embarrassed of her lunch box. She didn't want to take that thing out without me sitting there to block anyone's view of it. I don't know why she's so embarrassed about it 'cause it's the prettiest lunch box in the whole wide world. It's this pink plastic treasure chest thingy that reminds me of a box of Whitman's chocolates with a lid and all, but Sun Joo's lid got this cute rainbow on it, and it's got words, too. "Happiness is like the smile of a rainbow with colors that sparkle of joy and love." The girl's into rainbows.

She opens the lid, quickly tucks it under the box, and hovers over her food, hiding it.

"It's okay. I ain't going to take your food," I say, opening my chocolate milk.

"No, not like that," she says, and picks at her rice. She got chopsticks in the box, but she uses the school's spork instead.

The food in her lunch box is so neat it don't even look like real food. There's rice on one side of the box. Slices of pink blocks on the other side. Next to that are slices of yellow coin-looking thingies. I see strawberries tucked here and there. A boiled egg. It's like an art project.

"What's that there?" I ask, pointing at the pink blocks.

"Spam. You want?" she says, pushing the box toward me.

"Sure! Oh man, what you got looks way better than what I got," I say, pointing down at my tray of mashed potatoes, Salisbury steak, and mushy green beans all sopped with beige gravy. "You want to try some of this?" I ask.

She scoops up some mashed potatoes with gravy and tastes it. She nods and says, "Is not bad."

"You want to swap?" I ask.

"Swap?"

"Yeah. You know. Like trade. You get mine. I get yours. Swap," I say.

"Swap. Okay. We swap," she says.

With the tray of school lunch in front of her, Sun Joo sits up straight like she ain't embarrassed no more. I'm good at chopsticks, so I use her rainbow chopsticks, poking them into the rice.

"Did you make this?"

"No, my grandmother. She make," she says.

"Lucky duck," I say, chewing the rice. It's sweet and tangy.

"Duck?"

"Yeah, like quack-quack duck, but it ain't like quack-quack. It's just a saying. It means, like, I wish I had me what you have. I want me a grandma who packs me these kinds of lunches. This is like princess food. It is so yummy," I say, taking a bite of Spam.

She watches me eating up her food and says, "I think you are so friendly and so nice."

I smile so big the chewed-up Spam in my mouth nearly falls out. I swallow and then say, "Why, thank you, Sun Joo Moon. Thank you so much. That truly warms my heart. But I can't take all the credit for that 'cause you bring out the nice in me. You really do. You know how, like, some people just rub you all wrong and next thing you know you're fuming mad and all irritated and calling them names and you don't even know why? But you're nothing like that. You push all my nice buttons. You really do."

Sun Joo smiles and nods like she gets what I'm saying, but I don't know for sure 'cause I'm gabbing a mile a minute with no plans on stopping. I'm on a roll.

"But I'm afraid being nice don't get you too far in this neck of the woods, if you know what I'm saying. Like you kinda have to have a streak of mean if you're going to be somebody around here. I'm talking somebody with a capital *S*. You gotta have attitude. Like that girl Sydney. See her over there? See how she holds her nose up and swings her hair like that? It's like she's queen of the hill or something and the rest of us is a bunch of nobodies. You know, her friends nominated her for president. Oh man, I wish I had friends like that. Always right by my side. Nominating me. Following me around. Telling me how pretty I am. I think I'd make a great president. I got so many ideas to change this place up. I'd represent everyone, especially the nobodies. I'd help everyone. But for girls like Sydney, it's not about making the world a better place, it's not. It's all about

24

power and popularity. Want to hear something pathetic? I'm probably going to vote for her 'cause she's got that star power."

Sun Joo nods like she gets what I'm saying, but who knows 'cause her English ain't that great. She pulls an apple out of her rainbow backpack. She grips it with both hands like she's pressing hard on it, like she's trying to twist open a lid on a jar. Then crunch. Like magic, the apple splits in half. Sun Joo split that apple in half with her bare hands.

"Wow," I say.

She hands me half her apple. I take it. I look at it, making sure it's a real apple, and say, "Oh my tarnation, how'd you do that?"

She takes a bite and says, "Is my star power."

"Girl," I say, and hold my hand up for a high five.

She high-fives me back.

five

Ma's sleeping when me and Benny get back from school. We gotta keep it quiet. It's like we're sneaking into our own home. It's been like this since she started working nights regular.

Benny turns the TV on. I rush to push the mute button.

"But I can't hear nothing," Benny whispers, grabbing the remote from me.

"Can't you read lips?" I whisper back.

"I don't like reading," he says, and turns on the sound, but he keeps it low at one notch. He sits so close to the screen his face glows with the happy family splitting open a Hot Pocket. *What're you going to pick? Hot Pockets.* Benny licks his lips and swallows.

"You're going get blind," I tell him.

"I'm hungry."

I pick him up, set him a little farther away, and give him one more notch of volume.

"Didn't you have no lunch?"

"I want a sandwich."

"Hang on. I'll make you something," I say, and head over to the kitchen.

As I spread mayo on bread, I hear the TV get louder. I rush over, turn the volume down, bop Benny's head with the remote, and take it with me. We can't have us another blowup.

One time, we had the TV on too loud while Ma was sleeping, and she came storming and stumbling out of her room like a drunk-up maniac, yelling at us to keep it down and throwing whatever she could get her hands on. Cushions, hairbrush, stack of junk mail, ashtrays, a barrel of Cheese Balls that was open and full. Them balls went flying all over the living room, and Charlie went crazy jumping to catch them midair. Benny and him vacuumed those puffs up off the floor, crunching and munching on them like it was manna from the Father God Almighty himself. Food from heaven gave Charlie the runs. Woke up in the morning to the glorious view of Lake Orange Diarrhea at the front door. Guess who got to clean that up?

I struck it lucky Ma didn't run into Charlie's sick mess, 'cause she'd been threatening to get rid of him. Costs too much to keep him. (It don't cost that much.) He's getting old. (He's but like fifty years old in people age.) Too much work taking care of that oversize animal.

(I feed, water, and walk him. She don't lift a pinkie.)

Ma's spewing off sorry excuses 'cause Charlie was Daddy's idea from the get-go. He brought him home as a pup, and we went wild, falling in love. Ma's just rampaging to rid our home of any signs of Daddy.

I wish Ma had the wherewithal to give herself a time-out and think long and hard before she rampages, opening her big old mouth and erupting everything into a ruckus. One of these days she's going to break our TV, throwing that Mother's Day ceramic ashtray Benny made for her clear through the screen. It weighs a brick and looks like a deflated heart.

A wad of I Can't Believe It's Not Butter! melts in the pan. As it spreads and sizzles, I plop down a slice of bread, mayo-side up. I top it with a sheet of cheese, which sweats and goes soft in the middle. I blanket the liquefying cheese with another slice of mayo bread and flip it. The fried side glistens golden and crusty. Beats that nasty grease cheese at school. My mouth waters.

I give Benny his sandwich.

"Does it got loaf?" he asks.

"No."

"I want loaf."

"I want a thank-you."

"Thank you," he says, chomping a mouthful.

"Don't talk with your mouth full."

"But you said you wanted me to say thank you."

He chews, smiling like a demon child.

I stoop, snatch a bite, and hurry back to the kitchen. It takes a second for Benny to say "Hey!"

We got Steak-umms in the freezer, but that's our last three sheets of beef, which I need to save for dinner. Ma's been wanting meat. She's on the fast track to looking and sounding like that barking grandma in that Wendy's commercial looking for where the beef is at.

For tonight's dinner special at the Chez Michel, we will serve noodles de macaroni and crème de cheese topped with delicate sheets de Steak-ummlicious thinly carved to melt-in-your-mouth tender perfection.

I leave the meat in the freezer, but take out the empty Steak-umm box. I cut out the front with the picture of a sub overflowing with ribbons of meat, melted cheese, and fried onions. Just cutting up the box works up my spit.

Ma's up. She stumbles to the bathroom. The toilet flushes. She stumbles out and back to her bedroom. The door slams shut.

On the blank side of the Steak-umm postcard, I write in caps: OK LEE.

I know his address by heart. Rosewood Lane's got a fancy ring to it. So does Silver Spring. Sure beats living on a street called Thirty-Five. It's an ugly, odd number. Dirty thirty. Dive five. Try to stay alive.

I'm all set to write "urinal" answering his "who's there," and he'd come back with "urinal who," and I'd come back with "urinal heap of trouble perv" just like how we ping-ponged a million years ago, when I caught him in the girls' bathroom crying. I never did find out what was making him cry that day. I would never shed tears in school. Never. I'd give myself one of them snap-out-of-it talks and move on.

As my pen forms the first stroke of the letter *U*, it detours, turning into an *I* instead, and that's all it takes for me to gush:

I camped at Ocean City after you took off to your fancy new house. No hard feelings. You woulda liked our tent. Daddy showed up late, made a mess of things, then took off. He and Ma fought. World War III. Don't want to get into it, but I gotta tell someone, may as well be you. He was in his truck cleaning his gun with Benny sitting next to him. Gun went off. No one got hurt. But cops came. Get this. Daddy told the cops Benny did it. Blamed his kid so he don't look stupid. Don't get no lower than that. Bubble busted. Then we get a flat on the side of the road next to some cornfields and Charlie goes running into the street and almost gets hit. Screeching tires like you never

heard. It's a miracle we're all in one piece. How'd
your summer go? What's school like? Here's my
knock-knock answer: Chesterfield.

> *From the one and only,*
> *Yoo No Hoo (my Korean name)*
> *PS Made a new friend. A bona fide FOB. Why*
ain't it FOP?
> *PPS You still owe me a year's worth of braids.*

My words make me feel light as a feather and stiff
as a board, like I can levitate off the floor.

I put a pot of water on the stove for boiling the macaroni. I join Benny and Charlie on the floor and watch
TV. Jill hops on the couch behind me and settles on
my shoulder. Kelly snuggles onto my lap. I don't know
where Sabrina's at. Bet she's under my bed. Benny's
head rests on the nook of Charlie's neck. They could
pass for a two-headed dog. I drape my legs over Charlie.
We fit like pieces of a puzzle.

This here's the calm before the hurricane.

Any minute, that doorknob's going to turn, and who
knows what's going to come spilling out while she gets
herself together to mind a tollbooth all night. Wonder if
there's any chance of Daddy driving through her booth
again. That's how they met. I seen a picture of them
taken before I was born. Daddy looked like Daddy, but

I had to squint to see Ma. She used to be real good-looking. If that's what it costs, I ain't never having babies. Wonder if Ma wonders if Daddy will ever drive through her booth again. It took five drive-throughs for him to get her number. That's romance. Under all that raging, Ma's just real sad. Daddy ain't what we imagined he was. Hardly ever here for us to get a real feeling about him. We dreamed him up.

I think I fell prey to the dreaming harder than Ma and Benny did. It's just that every time I started spiraling down into that dark hole of doubting Daddy, he'd show up with a stuffed animal in one hand, a bouquet of flowers in the other, and that missed-you-to-the-moon-and-back smile that erased all those days I spent wondering where he was at and why he ain't here.

Ma hates me. I can feel it. It's 'cause I like Daddy better. When he did show, I was always like "Daddy this" and "Daddy that," always picking him over her, siding with him, when she was the one who was here steady for us. I think she resents me for that. I try. Lord knows I try with Ma, but it's so hard 'cause she's so darn grumpy. You ever try snuggling with a jagged rock? You get nothing but aches and bruises.

Working nights don't help none. She's so beat-up tired, and it's gotta be stranded-on-an-island lonely in that tollbooth. When she worked days, she'd be nice and normal to me, ask about school, give a hug here and there, offer me some motherly facts of life, get dinner together, laugh at Benny's antics, clean up some, snuggle with the cats, walk Charlie. . . . Working nights is sucking every ounce of nice out of her. It's like she's a vampire. But it's either that or bills don't get paid.

When we got back from Ocean City, Ma was talking to Great-Aunt Barb on the phone. She lives on the family farm in Ohio. I heard Ma say that if worse comes to worse, we'd have to head over there. She don't want to go back 'cause that's at least a hundred steps bass ackward, and she got bad memories and bad feelings. My grandparents died in a fire on that farm before my time. Ma got orphaned 'cause of that farm. She thinks she should've died that night, but she snuck out to meet up with her boyfriend. She was but sixteen years old. The way I see it: Her life got spared. The way she sees it: She should've been home to save them. To this day, she freaks out about fires, worrying about the Christmas tree catching or Benny playing with matches or the stove being on. It's a wonder she smokes so much.

The water boils, sizzling as it bubbles over into the flame. I climb out of our cuddle and go to the kitchen. I turn down the heat and dump two boxes of macaroni into the water. I save the boxes for future postcards.

Ma's doorknob jiggles.

six

As long as I don't flunk and do over a grade, I'm good. Ma and Daddy never said nothing about my report cards. Hardly ever got As. One or two Bs. Mostly Cs. One or two Ds. They didn't care as long as I didn't flunk. So my standard's always been: Just don't flunk.

I never got what the big whoop was about getting on honor roll and Principal's List. Ok was do-or-die about getting all As. He studied like his life was on the line. I hate studying. It's so boring. Just thinking about it makes me droopy, sad, and sleepy. Don't make no sense to memorize all that gibberish you ain't ever going to need in real life just so's you can get an A and get your name on a stupid list. Big old waste of ticktock, if you ask me. That's how I've always felt about schoolwork, so when Sun Joo asks me to help her study for the science vocab quiz, I'm like, "What? Excuse me?"

Honest to angels, I don't know how much help I can give her 'cause I ain't the studying type, but my English is way better than hers, so I take her to the library during recess to learn her some science words.

I pull Sun Joo to the way back of the library and sit her down on the floor in an aisle of bookshelves. She got geography books behind her. I got history books behind me. It smells musty like old newspapers. Smell of cinnamon's in the air too, 'cause of Ms. Davenport, our librarian. I like her. She ain't nothing like your run-of-the-mill librarian. She's all hippie with long flowing skirts, a nose piercing, a READ tattoo on her wrist, and the scent of cinnamon following wherever she goes. Only problem is she's real pushy about pushing books. She tried to turn me on to reading. I said no thank you.

Sun Joo pulls out what looks like a miniature pocket Bible with tissue-paper pages. It's her Korean–English dictionary. Around her wrist is a freshly braided rainbow friendship bracelet.

"Where'd you get that?" I ask.

"I make it," she says.

"I like that. That's so pretty. I'll bet that took forever," I say, turning her wrist to get a better look at the colors.

"Thanks. Is not forever," she says, pulling out a stack of flash cards.

"What you got there? Your backpack's full of all sorts of goodies. Let me see those," I say.

She hands the cards to me. These are like the beauty-pageant winner of flash cards. Sky-blue index cards with the American words in green marker. There's some Korean writing in red. On the back side is the meaning of the word in purple with a little drawing of whatever the science thing is. Her letters are so perfect they look typed.

"Sun Joo, you made these?"

She nods.

"You need to show these to Ms. T. You'd get an A right off the bat. That part's Korean, right?" I ask.

She nods.

"What's it mean?"

"It mean same thing. That one help me say it."

"So this here's 'cell' in Korean."

"Yes. Cell."

"Oh, cool. I like how that looks. It's just a cluster of sticks. It's kind of amazing how you can write the same sounds with a bunch of sticks, you know? You going to have to show me how you do that. Okay, back to work. So, what's a cell?"

"Um. I know it. It is the smallest of all functional and structural unit of all the living organism," she says slowly.

"Bingo. You got that right word for word. You memorized all that?"

"I have to do it."

"No, you just have to have an idea. Get the key words down. It's probably going to be a multiple-choice thing anyway. You can eeny meeny miny mo it and still pass," I say.

"Eeny meeny?" she asks.

"Yeah, take a guess. You know, pick whatever."

"No. I can't do like that."

"Whatever floats. Work hard or work smart. I choose to work smart. Okay, next word is 'nucleus.' What's a nucleus?"

"How do you say?"

"Nucleus."

"Nu. Cre. Us."

"Close enough. So what's it mean?"

"Nucleus is brain of cell. It the control place of cell. It have all the DNA," she says.

"This here says control center, but control center, control place, same difference. I'll give it to you," I say.

"Control center. Okay. I remember center."

"Next. What's a vacuole?"

"What you say?"

"Vacuole."

"Let me see," she says, and looks at her card. "Uh. *Beh koo oh*. How you say?"

"Vacuole."

"Behcure."

"Follow my lips. Bite down first. Vaaaaa," I say, sounding like a sheep.

She bites down on her lower lip and says, "Vaaaa."

"You got it. Now say 'keeewwww,'" I say, puckering up like I'm a goldfish about to give a kiss.

"Kuuuu," she says, puckering back.

"Ohhhhhllll," I say.

"Ohhhh," she says.

"Ohhhh luh. Do like this. Ohhhh luh," I say, reaching for her jaw.

"Ohhh luh," she says, as I squeeze her chin and open it down.

"Now put it together. Vacuole," I say.

"Behcure," she says.

"You going to need to practice that. But she ain't testing for pronunciation. You don't need to worry about it."

"But I want to say right," she says.

"You'll get it. This stuff takes time. Just hang with me. I'll get you talking good in no time," I say.

"Thank you for help," she says.

"You bet. Okay, back to work. What's a vacuole?"

"Vaaaa cu ohhh luh. It store everything. It store the food, the water, the waste, the mineral," she says.

"That's right. It looks like a big glob. Okay, next is Golgi body? Is it Gol jee? Gol gee? You know?"

"I think it Gol jee. That's how Ms. T say. Gol jee. But

gogi is Korean word too, you know. Gogi. It mean the meat. You know, like eating the meat."

"You mean like a gogi ball sub or a gogi loaf?"

Sun Joo scrunches her brows, so I explain, "Like meatball and meat loaf."

"Uhhh. Yes, I like the meat loaf," she says, nodding.

"Speaking of gogi, I'm hungry," I say.

"I have to say what the Golgi body mean. It mean where inside cell you sort and pack the protein inside the vesicle. It look like the many rubber bands together," she says.

"Sun Joo, you work too hard," I say.

"Did I get right?"

"You got it, but you work too hard."

"I have to do perfect."

"No, you don't. Good enough is good enough."

"But I need perfect because I am sooooo behind. I feel, like, sooooo stupid here because my English is sooooo bad. Everybody, they laugh," she says.

"Who laughed at you?"

"Everybody. Except you. I'm so embarrass."

"What happened? Why'd they laugh at you?"

"In the English class. I need the paper, and I ask the teacher for the sheet of paper, but I say the bad word because I don't say right 'the sheet,' and everyone laugh because the other one is the bad word."

"Oh. You said the S word? You said that? To the teacher? Oh, that's funny. That's, like, gold, girl," I say.

"What you mean 'gold'?"

"It's good. It's pure. It's like gold. That right there could get everyone to like you and think you're cool. But you have to act like you know what's up, like you know what you're doing, so they're laughing with you, not at you. So here's how I do when people laugh at me. I just laugh right along and pretend like I made all that fun happen on my terms. That's how you take your power back," I say.

"I don't know if I can do," she says.

"You can do. Say it. Say 'I can do.'"

"I can do."

"Keep saying it. I can do. I can do."

"I can do. I can do," we whisper-chant together until we bust out laughing.

"Shhhh. Quiet," I say.

We stare at each other. We hear the wheels of Ms. Davenport's book cart squeak down the next aisle.

"Hey, Sun Joo," I whisper.

"Hey, Mickey?" she whispers back.

"Show me how you write my name in Korean. Here. Put it over here," I say, giving her my palm.

She holds my hand steady as she presses her pen into my palm. It tickles. When she's done, she shows my name to me. Pointing at the first set of sticks, she says, "That is 'Mi.' And that is 'Ki.' Mi. Ki."

I stare at it and say, "So that right there is, like, a box and a stick, then that right there is, like, a backward *F* and a stick. That is so cool. I love this. I'm going to cherish this. I ain't never washing this hand," I say.

"That's gross, but whatever floats," she says.

"Listen to you. Ain't you funny."

The bell rings.

"Meet me at lunch. Same table," I say, getting up.

"Okay," she says, and follows me down the aisle of books.

We walk out of the library into the hall already crowded with kids. I know Sun Joo's got math now, so I grab her hand and pull her along to her classroom so she don't get lost and trampled on. I tell her to stay close to me. I can feel her leaning into my backpack. Her hand fits so small in mine it's like I'm tugging Benny along. She squeezes my hand like she's scared or something. "Coming through. Coming through!" I shout, straightening my back and pushing through the bustle. Something about helping someone more lost and smaller than me gives me the feeling of being big and important. Like I'm somebody.

seven

First thing in the morning, I go to my locker and find me a surprise. It's a note. A rainbow envelope with my name on it. In Korean. A box and a stick next to a backward *F* and a stick. This makes me hop like a bunny, smile so big, and feel so happy, I nearly hug Kevin McDaniel, who's trying to open his locker next to me.

"Look what I got," I say, waving the envelope at him.

He don't even look up, but I don't care. I open the note. On matching rainbow paper, it says:

Dear Mickey,

Thank you for helping me. You are my good friend. Here is the present for you. Can you come to my home? We have the harvest celebration. It is so fun. My family say you can come. Please come if you like to.

Your friend,
Sun Joo

Folded inside the note, there's something bumpy wrapped in tissue paper. I'm so excited. No one's ever done nothing special like this for me. I open the present, and there it is. I gasp. It's a matching rainbow friendship bracelet, same as the one that Sun Joo has on. It's so pretty. The colors beam so bright, it's glowing up the entire hallway.

My eyes tear up, and you know how I feel about crying at school. I put the bracelet on my wrist, but I can't tie it by myself. I look around to see if anyone might help me. At the end of the hall around the corner, I see Sun Joo's little head peeping out. I wave to her. *Come here. Come here.*

She weaves her way through the hall, trying not to bump into anyone. Once she's close enough, I grab and pull her over to my locker. I hug and lift her up, shaking her. She feels light and flimsy like a rag doll. Her legs swing back and forth like the tail of a My Little Pony.

"Thank you so much," I say, putting her down. "This is so special to me. I'm going to treasure this so much for the rest of my life. This feels better than biting into a warm apple pie with a scoop of vanilla ice cream. You really made my day, Sun Joo."

"Okay," she says, clapping and bobbing.

"Here. Tie it for me," I say, holding out my wrist.

43

She double knots it nice and tight. I close my locker. We head down the hall together side by side. I bump her. She rubs her shoulder and says, "Owwww. That hurt."

"It did not," I say.

She smiles and bumps me back, to which I throw myself against the wall and say, "Owwwwww!"

She laughs. I love making her laugh. I keep remembering how sad she was under those stairs all by herself, and look at her now. I put my arm around Sun Joo and ask her about this harvest celebration at her place.

"It's the Chuseok."

"The chew what?"

"Chuseok."

"You mean like chew, as in 'chew the fat,' and suck, as in 'suck it up'?"

"Huh?"

"Chew the fat? You never heard of that? It means gabbing. You know, like talking on and on and on, blah, blah, blah, sit around and chitchat, yappity-yap, shoot the breeze."

"Like you do?"

"Ha-ha. Yeah, like I do. And suck it up means, like, 'stop belly aching and stop whining like a baby and keep on trucking,'" I say.

"That make sense. I like it," she says.

"'Chuseok' is easy to remember. So Chuseok's like a

party? Is there going to be games and dancing and all that fun stuff? What do you do there?"

"You can just come. Is fun. You eat food, and you meet everyone, and you chew the fat," she says.

"That's my girl," I say, and give her a high five.

"So you come?"

"I'd love to. It's my honor. Wouldn't miss it for all the tea in China, and don't go telling me you ain't Chinese 'cause I know you ain't. I know you're from Korea, from South Korea, not the North, which is run by a dictator who's starving people to death. I know my Koreas."

"Mickey?"

"Yeah?"

"Shhh."

eight

I'm in homeroom, standing next to Frankie Dooley and saying the Pledge of Allegiance, when I notice him picking his nose at the part about being under God, indivisible, with liberty and justice for all. I shake my head.

"What's up, Lions?"

Voices boom through the speaker.

"I'm Elijah. I'm Sydney S. Today is September nineteenth. At the top of the news: Nominations are in for the SGA elections! Here are the nominations! Y'all ready for this?"

Names get called out for secretary. Some I know. Some I don't. Names get called for treasurer. These are the kids who're good at math. Names get called for vice president. It's now turning into a popularity contest. Clapping and cheering follow the nominations. I feel queasy with envy.

"Now for the nominations for president. Y'all ready

for this? Drumroll, please. With the most nominations, we have . . . yours truly! Sydney Stevenson! Thank you! Runner up is Jack Martell! Randall Robinson! And last and least, with one nomination, there's Mickey McDonald. Congratulations! Good luck on your campaigns! Vote for Sydney. Just kidding. Not really. May the best Lion win! And don't forget, today after school there will be . . ."

Hearing my name over the speaker makes the room spin. Did I get that right? Was I dreaming? Did I really hear Sydney say my name? My heart races. I breathe so heavy I'm fogging up the windows and flapping the American flag above the chalkboard. Am I dreaming? I forget it's Frankie sitting next to me, and I tap his arm and ask, "You hear that? Did she say my name? Who put me in?"

Frankie side-eyes me, grins all sneaky, and whispers, "I did. Will you marry me?"

"Don't be gross. Go back to picking your nose."

His ears turn red. Covering his creepy smile, he tells me to shut up.

"Better be nice to me, 'cause I'm going to be president. I'm winning this thing."

nine

Sun Joo did it. She was the one who nominated me. I never thought she had it in her to do something like write my name on the nomination board, but she did just 'cause I mentioned how lucky Sydney was to have friends nominating her. I never had a best friend before, but that right there is what BFF is all about. I told her she's my campaign manager, my right-hand girl, my go-to, my sidekick. I don't know if she knew what I meant, but she nodded and bounced all excited. We even came up with our own signature handshake. It goes patty-cake, patty-cake, slap, slap, bump the fists, and wiggle the fingers to a high ten.

I'm running against Jack Martell the jock and Randall Robinson, a regular diner at the all-you-can-achieve restaurant, and the one and only Sydney Stevenson, the captain of the Head Over Hills Step Team.

I strut down the hall, passing vote-for-me posters taped to the walls. I couldn't buy no real poster boards, so I used the back of leftover wrapping paper, which ended up being easier to cut, carry, and tape to the walls. I found me a fridge box at the dumpster and made a cartoon cutout of myself with big hair, roller skates, one fist on hip, the other holding up a pickax, and a big bubble coming out of my mouth saying my slogan "Mick's Your Pick!"

My cutout's standing at the end of the hall. I'm mighty proud as a peacock. I got a good stab at this. Even if I lose, I win, 'cause anyone who's anyone at this school's going to know who I am. *Hey, there goes Mickey! Aren't you Mickey? It's Mickey!* I'm not aiming to be popular. Not like that. I'm just aiming not to disappear off the face of this earth, 'cause sometimes I can feel the fade of death and insignificance. It's like I'm slowly but surely vanishing off and away to the Island of the Invisibles.

I want nothing to do with being invisible.

Look at me! Look at me!

I catwalk like I'm on a runway. Today's outfit consists of a navy-blue T-shirt and a white skirt I made from an old pillowcase. All's I had to do was cut open the closed end, and bingo was her name-o, I had me a white skirt like the ones secretaries and stewardesses wear. I finished off the outfit with a red headband and a red belt I fashioned from an onion sack.

As I pass the lockers, the Red Sea of voters parts. I smile and nod. I'm on tip-top of the world. Maybe not just yet, but I'm well on my way, making my dreams come true. Nothing ain't going to stop me from nothing. Mickey McDonald's making her mark. As I strut, I feel like sprouting wings, flying high, and flowing through the sky.

Then I feel something that stops me in my tracks.

I freeze.

I can't take another step.

I can't move, 'cause if I move, the big blood booger that just gooped out of my Private Regina is going to streak down my legs, and this ain't the pop of color I was aiming for. This ain't the flow I was talking about.

Everyone's moving around me. Voices chatter. Lockers open and shut. Feet patter. Kids laugh. Bell rings. Hall spins. The world blurs.

I got my period?

I got my period.

I got my period!

Why's it called period? It should be called exclamation point, 'cause that's what I'm feeling right now, like I should exclaim, "I got my period!" It's a real headliner of a news flash. I've been waiting for this, but now? Not now. Why now? I ain't prepared. I got no sanitary protection.

This ain't how I imagined my inauguration into womanhood.

My periodic/exclamatory dream was I'd wake up in the morning to the glorious stains of womanhood on my panties and sheets, and I'd have some precious alone time to gaze upon the stains like they were clouds in the sky. This one looks like a dolphin. This one's a rosebud. I see me the explosion of fireworks on the Fourth of July. Ain't that fitting? My own personal declaration of independence.

But my dream has been rudely slashed, and I see Lawrence Elwood stop at my cardboard figure. He laughs, throwing his head back, his hair swooshing like a wave of wishing. He looks down the hall and sees me. Split-second eye contact is all he needs to make his way over here with his head of good hair and a smile that's reminding me of candles on a birthday cake.

I need to get my behind to a bathroom ASAP. Pressing my knees together, I slide. I want to think I look like I'm gliding, but it probably looks more like hobbling.

Go away, Lawrence Elwood. Go away.

"Hey, Mickey," he says.

"Hi," I say with my thighs pressed tight and my back turned to the lockers.

"That's hilarious."

"Thanks."

"It's a trident reference?"

"Trident? You mean like the gum?"

"Like the myth."

"What're you talking about, Lawrence?"

"Could you call me Law?"

"Law?"

"Yeah, it's short for Lawrence."

"Like Law as in law-abiding citizen?"

"More like Law as in law of attraction."

He smiles like he just blew out all his birthday candles in one huff-and-puff.

I'm normally whip quick with my comebacks, but I'm flustered. Heat's rising from my chest, running up my neck and setting my cheeks on fire. Lawrence Elwood is flirting with me, and I got nothing. With burnt brain cells, I blurt out, "Well, whoop-de-do, Larry. I hope you're attracted to voting for me 'cause Mick's your pick."

I shimmy away from him faster than a cockroach seeing light.

I dodge bodies, hurrying to the bathroom.

I see the top of Sun Joo's head. I reach over, grab her arm, pull her to me, and tell her I got me an emergency and haul her to the bathroom with me.

When we finally make it there, I show her my back-side and ask, "See anything?"

"Oh no," Sun Joo says, covering her mouth and step-ping away from me like I got some contagious disease.

"What?"

"You have the menses."

"The men what?"

"You not know?"

"Not know what?"

"Your mother not say?"

"Say what?"

"About the menses."

"*Menseh?* What in tarnation is menseh? Are you talking about menstruation? Is that what you call it? No one calls it that around here. It's lady business or that time of month or Aunt Flo, have your pick, but no one says 'menstruation' or 'menses,' 'cause guess what—men don't see nothing."

That word gets me started on a rant about why in tarnation the word "men" is in a thing that's all about being a woman. It should be called womenstruation. But why in tarnation is the word "man" in the word "woman"? And why in tarnation is "male" in "female"? What's that all about? They got no business. They want in on everything. Putting their names and noses in places they don't belong. Don't even get me started.

While I'm ranting, Sun Joo covers her eyes and turns her back to me, trying to give me my privacy.

"I don't care. I don't need privacy. What I need right now is a pad. You got a pad?" I ask.

She unzips the front pocket on her backpack, pulls out a Care Bear pouch, unzips that, pulls out another pouch, unzips that, pulls out another pouch. It's like a Russian doll of pouches. Finally, she pulls out a pad all wrapped in pink plastic decorated with flowers. She holds it up like it's some treasure she dug up out of the ground and hands it to me.

"You, Sun Joo Moon, are my sunshine," I say, hurrying into a stall.

While I'm taking care of my lady business, I sing, "'You make me happy when skies are gray. You'll never know dear, how much I love you'—oh my Lord of Lords, Sun Joo, this pad's got wings. I think this baby's going to fly. You ever see that commercial? All them pretty women look so happy to be on the rag—'Please don't take my sunshine away.'"

As I step out of the stall, I ask, "You know that song?"

Sun Joo takes her sweater off and starts wrapping it around my waist to cover the stain on my skirt.

"I ain't wearing this. It messes up my outfit. This thing's so small. What is it, like newborn size? Besides, I got nothing to hide. I ain't ashamed of my period," I say.

"Noooooooo," she says, shaking her head.

"Yeeeessss," I say, nodding my head.

"No, this not good for you."

"Listen up, Sun Joo. From the bottom of my heart of hearts, I truly am grateful for all your help. You saved my butt, but I do things my way, and hiding my womanly stains ain't the Mickey way. This here's a natural bodily function for every woman. News flash! This here's a miracle. Without it, we can't have no babies. Without it, all of humanity goes to extinction. So I see this here as a point of pride. Why should I hide? Why should I be ashamed? You getting what I'm saying?"

"But it look like you poo-poo," she says.

"Oh. It does?"

"No one vote for you like this."

"You think so?"

"No one want President Poo-Poo."

"Well, I guess that's a good point."

"Take this. Take this out," she orders, untucking my T-shirt from my pillowcase skirt. She pulls the shirt down, turns me around, and says, "Too short. You have jacket?"

"No."

"Why you wearing white today?"

I check my butt out in the mirror. It does look more like poo than blood.

"Hey, it kinda looks like South America, don't it?" I say.

Sun Joo turns my skirt around this way and that, inspecting me up, down, and side to side, then claps her hands with an excitement I never seen coming from Her Highness Shyness, and announces, "I know! I solve! I have the perfect idea!"

She pushes me back into the stall, telling me to take my skirt off and give it to her. I can't say no. I can't say wait. She's pushy like some used-car salesman. This a side of her I ain't ever seen before. I hand her my skirt under the stall door. She snatches it. Next thing I hear is rummaging. I peek through the crack. Sun Joo's opening up one of her magical pouches. She's getting something, but I can't tell what.

"Hey, Sun Joo? What you up to over there? Might I kindly remind you that that there's my property, and I got rights, and I should most certainly have a say, if not *the* say, in how you planning to fix this situation? I sure do hope you ain't aiming to wash my article of clothing, 'cause I sure as heaven ain't going to wear a wet skirt all over school. What's worse? People thinking you got a smudge of poo on your butt or people thinking you peed yourself? If you ask me—"

"Be quiet."

"Be what? Are you telling me to shut up?"

"Yes."

"Well, I never. Excuse me, little missy Moon, this here's a hostage situation. I want my skirt back. How do I know you ain't going to just walk out of here and abandon me and leave me stuck in this here stall for the rest of my life all alone and destitute without food and clothing. See what you done now? You got me thinking about my daddy and what—"

My skirt comes flying over the stall door. I shut up and catch it. I hold it up. I gasp like I just walked in on my surprise birthday party. Surprise! I can't breathe 'cause what my friend's done for me just takes my breath away.

"Oh my Lord of Lords, Sun Joo! This here's a work of art."

We strut down the hall. Well, I don't know if Sun Joo's walk can be considered strutting, but she ain't staring down at the floor all full of the trembles. She throws her rainbow backpack of magical pouches over one shoulder and walks like she belongs, like she got rights, like she's proud of what she's done to my skirt.

She whipped up the whole wide world.

With whatever Magic Markers and pens and paints and pastels she had stashed in one of her pouches, she turned that stain into South America, drawing around it a globe of the world: North America, a chunk of Greenland, some Africa, a piece of Europe and the beautiful oceans, Pacific and Atlantic, done in presidential blue.

It got me humming that tune about how God's got the whole world in his hands, but truth be told, I got the whole world on my right hip.

ten

Instead of the usual tube socks I wear with my roller skates, I'm wearing Ma's Sheer Energy knee-highs brought to you by L'eggs 'cause my feet wouldn't slip in. My toes are squished. I'm praying the seams don't bust when Principal Farmer calls my name and I got to stand up and roll over to the podium to give my vote-for-me speech in front of the entire school.

I'm nervous.

It's like I got billions of butterflies in my gut, and if I open my mouth, they're going to come flying out. Maybe that's just what I need, my turn to open my mouth, my turn to speak and let the butterflies out.

I silently practice my speech. The sweat on my hands makes my note cards damp and soft, smudging up my words.

Jack Martell's doing the talking right now. He got on his basketball outfit—a pair of shorts and a jersey tank top with MARTELL and the number "13" on his back. It takes a heap of nerves to wear unlucky thirteen with such joy and pride. It's like he's too strong for bad luck. He wears it like a dare. Me, on the other hand, don't think too highly of thirteen. I'm hanging on to twelve for as long as I can. Two more months and it's bye-bye to my childhood. Hello to the teen scene. This must be what bittersweet feels like, winning and losing at the same time.

Ain't nothing going to be simple no more. It used to be that I didn't give half a hoot about what other people thought of me. Caring about how others saw me didn't even cross my mind. I did as I was led by none other than myself. If I felt like dancing, I danced. If I felt like singing, I sang. If I felt like skipping to my Lou, I skipped. Now I try hard not to care. That trying-hard part means I do mind. I do care what they think of me. It's not innocent no more.

Jack says something about wanting more dances, more soda machines, free fries on Fridays, and a longer lunch period, which I think is a horrible idea for those folks who don't got no friends and no food and nowhere to go. I'd say open up the library or the art room or some other classroom that don't make them feel like gum stuck on a shoe when they walk in.

Then he talks about how he plays ball. He's on a

team. He's good at working together. He wants to work with us to make this the best year.

"For the win!" he shouts, and holds up his open hands. Someone in the audience throws him a basketball. He catches it and spins it on his finger.

Kids go wild.

Jack leans into the mic, says, "Vote for Jack. He's got your back," and throws the ball into the audience.

Everyone gasps. Who's going to catch it?

My feet are numb. Blood ain't circulating past my ankles.

Sydney Stevenson is up next. She's wearing her step outfit. Her hair is amazing. I want her hair. It's dark brown, long, wavy, full of body, sheen, and shine. It's what I call wig perfect. She could sell shampoo.

She sashays to the podium, pulls the mic out of the stand, and says, "While Jack's busy catching balls, I'm going to tear down walls. Walls that divide. Walls that blind. Walls blocking minds. Here's the real catch. I'm your match. With President Stevenson, we, Lions, will be flying."

She drops the mic and does a backflip, finishing with the splits. Ouch. But, oh my Lord of Lords, I want to vote for her so bad. I crazy applaud. I'd stand, too, but my feet are too numb.

While Randall Robinson gets called to the podium,

I loosen my laces. I try to wiggle my toes, but they ain't budging. I gotta get these off, or I'm going to end up inch-worming my way to the mic.

I grab my left skate and pull. Nothing. I pull again. Nothing. It's stuck on my foot like a block of cement. Grabbing the wheels, I pull hard like I'm tugging on the horns of a bull eyeing Little Red Riding Hood. Oh no you don't. The skate pops off. My foot's finally free, and so is the skate.

It twirls in the air like a juggler's bowling pin.

I spring out of my metal folding chair so fast and hard it topples back and shuts, clanking onto the floor. My note cards fly out of my hands. I roll on the one skate still on my foot. I fall flat on my belly. I slide across the stage like I'm stealing home for the win. I put my hand out. The runaway skate falls into my palm.

What a catch.

Kids make a ruckus.

This all happens just in time for Randall Robinson to reach the podium, turn to see me sprawled across the stage, and say into the mic, "Thank you for the introduction."

"Ladies and gents, Randall Robinson," I say.

Kids laugh.

I stand up, dust myself off, hold my head high, and

hobble back with presidential dignity. I open my chair and take a seat.

"Ready to roll?" Randall says.

Kids applaud.

He swiped my opening line. My aim was to skate, spin, and twirl to the podium and ask the audience if we was ready to roll. What in tarnation am I going to say now? My sorry soggy note cards are scattered all across who knows where down there beneath the stage, and I gotta come up with a speech.

Randall's real serious. He wears his Easter Sunday best—a navy suit, a white shirt, and a necktie covered in red, white, and blue candy-cane stripes. He ain't just running to be president of a middle school. This here's the practice run to rule the country someday. Randall talks all grown-up. He uses big words like "represen-tation," "constituent," "dissatisfaction," "inalienable rights," blah, blah, blah. I guess it's impressive and all, but I'm fighting the yawns. He's talking about how he got credentials up the wazoo 'cause he makes all As on his report cards, runs the newspaper, runs the fastest mile, blah, blah, blah. Randall's a big bore. Kids must think so too 'cause there's so much restless mumble-jumble going on out there that Vice Principal Graves has to take the mic.

"Settle. Settle," he says.

Makes me think of them early Pilgrim settlers and how Thanksgiving's around the corner. Wonder how things'll play out this year with Daddy gone and all. Ma usually cooked up a storm. Daddy usually made it home to eat with us.

Knock, knock.

Who's there?

Wilma.

Wilma who?

Wilma cook a turkey this year?

"Settle down!" Graves howls, his spit spraying the podium, his lips touching all over the mic. Yuck. Pass the Lysol.

"Thank you, Vice Principal Graves. In conclusion, I am the best man for the job. I am the most qualified. If voted your president, I promise to serve and represent Landover Hills with the dignity, commitment, and hard work you deserve. Vote for me," he says.

No one claps. We ain't sure if he's done yet.

He clears his throat and says, "For a job well done, vote Robinson."

Randall didn't finish that quite right. The audience applauds, but it don't sound like how it sounded after Jack's and Sydney's speeches. Like you clap 'cause you gotta clap. It's pity-plause. Randall's got all the creds, but he feels too much like being at church.

"Last but not least, Michaela McDonald," Principal Farmer says.

My turn. I roll on the one skate. I get to the podium and say, "It's Mickey. Mickey as in the Mouse? And McDonald as in Happy Meals. My mouth's watering, so I'm going to make this quick 'cause we're all hungry for lunch.

"First off, I want to thank my very best friend, Sun Joo Moon, 'cause she nominated me. Y'all don't know her 'cause she's brand-new to our school. By golly, she's brand-new to America. She moved here all the way from South Korea. That's, like, on the other side of the ocean. I know a lot of you came from other countries too. Well, I was born and raised right here, so I can't even imagine what a heap of trouble that must've been. I'm really glad you're here, 'cause if you weren't, you wouldn't be able to vote for me," I say, wishing so bad I had wings, 'cause I'm running out of things to say, which never happens to me. If I had wings, I'd flap them open right about now and glide across the auditorium. Everyone would ooooh and ahhhh, and I'd fly out the window, up, up, and away.

"Ummm. If I become president, I'm going to make sure no one goes hungry, and ummm, everyone has a friend, you know, like a buddy system, and ummmm, everyone has school supplies like pens and pencils and paper, and ummm, as your president, I promise to give you my Tater Tots. No, I'm just kidding about the Tater Tots. For real though, as your president, I promise to do my best and give you my absolute ultimate. So Vote Mickey McDonald 'cause Mick's your pick. Thank you," I say, and roll on my one skate back across the stage.

The kids applaud. It's not as rowdy as the applause Sydney and Jack #13 got, but it's louder than what they gave Randall Robinson.

It don't matter if it's a thousand pairs of hands or one. I love applause. Something about the sound of all that clapping feeds my soul. I was aiming to roll back to my seat, but when I get to center stage, I so badly want to do something fancy, like a twirl or a spin, but with one skate, it's impossible. So I just bend at the waist, open my arms like wings, and lift my other leg back, skating to my chair like I'm a butterfly.

I miss my seat. I roll right past it. I'm heading for the edge of the stage. I know I have to stop now or it's off the cliff I go, but I don't want to stop. I lean my weight in, and off I fly. I spring off the stage, rolling into the sunset. It's not even a nanosecond, but it feels like a flash of forever. I stick my landing, skate out the doors into the empty hall, where I spin like Kristi Yamaguchi finishing up her routine, spinning and spinning like the final cycle on a washing machine, wringing out every last drop of sadness. I'm spinning so strong I sprout wings and lift off the floor, ceilings opening wide. Like a shooting star, I zoom straight to heaven, where Daddy and Ma are friends again. They're holding hands, and Benny's sitting on Daddy's shoulders, eating a ham sandwich with crumbs falling onto Daddy's hair, and Charlie's barking and our cats meow-meow, cheering me on.

I wish.

eleven

Here's what really happens: I fall off the stage. I land all wrong. I thought I knew how to fall right, but I crash, face-first onto the linoleum floor. Then I slide like I'm riding a Slip 'n Slide, except there ain't no water, no sunshine, no fun, just a metal door at the end of the rainbow, where my head rams. Hard. I'm hurting. *Breathe. Breathe. Get up. Get up.* My throbbing face is sopping wet. Am I crying? These ain't tears. This here's blood, gushing out of my nose, my mouth, my eyes, my ears. I can't even tell where all this blood is coming from. I taste metal. The room spins. Ms. Larkin hovers over me, her rhinestone earrings dangling like Christmas. The voice of Vice Principal Graves pounds in my head. He yells at everyone to "sit, sit, sit, settle, settle, settle," 'cause the kids are oooooohing and aaahhhhing and ewwwwwing as they move in on me to get a closer look at the blood and gore.

This butterfly is going to butter-cry, get stomped on, and butter-die if she don't get herself up.

I sit up, holding my face, blood oozing out between my fingers.

"Stay put, child," Ms. Larkin says, giving me a wad of paper towels. Feels like sandpaper against my face.

I slowly rise.

"You sure?" she says, holding my arm.

I stand up. I hear applause. The kids clap for me.

Ms. Larkin grabs Asa off the wall and tells him to walk me to the nurse's office.

As I limp out the door, I raise my bloody hand and give everyone a wave.

The metal door shuts behind Asa and me. The hall is quiet. The ruckus from the cafeteria sounds like it's coming from the apartment next door. They're having a party. I hobble. My wheels sound like a baby rattle. Asa's hand is on my back, I guess so he can catch me quick if I fall. It's barely touching me, but I know it's there.

"Man," he says.

"I ain't a man."

"Woman, that was wreck."

"I think I lost a tooth."

"No way."

"Look," I say, stopping in the hall. I take the bloody

69

paper towels off my face and show him my teeth 'cause I can't believe the hole my tongue keeps poking through, and I need me a witness.

"Yeah, it's lost," he says.

"I think I swallowed it. You think the tooth fairy would mind a poopy tooth?"

"That's nasty," Asa says, chuckling. "You still believe in the tooth fairy?"

"I do."

"You do-do?"

I burst out laughing so hard I almost fall backward. Asa's hand steadies me. We're at the nurse's door. He opens it.

"Thanks," I say, walking in.

"You got my vote," he says, patting my shoulder.

I don't know what it is, but when Asa says that, I get this huge knot in my throat and my eyes pool up with tears. I hide my face behind the bloodied wad of paper towels so he can't see how his kindness is making me cry.

The door shuts. Nurse Hyde rushes over, puts her arm around me, and says, "What happened, baby?"

"I fell," I say, sniveling like a toddler.

She sits me down on one of them bench-looking beds covered with white tracing paper, which reminds me of the time in kindergarten we outlined our bodies on the same kind of paper and drew whatever outfit our hearts desired. I made myself Miss America with a tiara, a princess dress, a sash, and a bouquet of flowers. The teacher cut them out and taped them up all around the classroom so it was like everyone was holding hands in a big circle.

"Let me have a look," she says.

While Nurse Hyde cleans and bandages my wounds and dries my tears and takes the skate off my foot, with not one word of how stupid and thoughtless and selfish I am, how I'm such a hog for attention, how this here's going to cost us an arm and a leg, how we're going to have to give Charlie away, how this here's the kind of thing that drove Daddy to the hills . . . I wish to the heavens she were my ma. I know it's mean, but that's what I wish. I keep thinking if Ma were more like Nurse Hyde, maybe Daddy wouldn't have left us. I get it. I get how he wanted to leave. I want to go away too. If I had me a big truck to drive into the sunset, I'd leave Ma too.

But what I don't get is how in the heckers he could leave me.

twelve

It's late Sunday afternoon. Monday's creeping in on us. We need clean clothes for the week, so me and Ma walk two baskets full of dirty laundry over to the washer room in another apartment building on the other side of the creek.

"Ouch," I say 'cause I keep stepping on holly leaves. They prick at my feet like tacks.

"Why didn't you wear shoes?" Ma asks.

"'Cause they're falling apart, and I'm trying to make them last as long as I can 'cause you need your smokes. That's why," I say. But honest to angels, I just didn't feel like bothering, so I came out barefoot.

Ma don't say nothing. She keeps walking. I hate it when she don't come back with a jab 'cause it makes me feel so lousy. I step on the holly leaves to make myself feel worse.

"I'm working on it. I got overtime. We might have

something left over this month. I'll have you know I'm trying to quit," she says.

"Your job?"

"No. I can't quit my job. You want to be camping in the woods? I meant smoking. I'm aiming to quit smoking. I wish I could quit this job," she says.

"Well, it's about time you quit those cigs 'cause that's a early death sentence. They are. And not just for the one who's doing the smoking, but for the loved ones getting the secondhand fumes. Yeah, Ma, me and Benny and all our animals, we might die of lung cancer 'cause of you. You ever think about that?"

"I do. All the time. That's why I'm trying to quit, Mickey. How about a little cheerleading?"

"Rah-rah for Ma."

"Bite me, why don't you?" she says, and stops. She puts down the basket and rummages through our dirty clothes. She pulls out a pair of socks and holds them out, telling me to put them on.

"They're smelly," I say.

"They're yours. Beats getting your feet cut up and infected. Last thing we need's an ER visit," she says, tosses the socks at me, and gets back to walking.

I put them on, and it does feel better to walk. I hurry to catch up to her and say, "You should know Benny needs shoes more than I do."

We get to the laundry room. Dryers tumble. Washers shake. It smells like Downy fabric softener. I love this smell.

"Try and get it all in one load," Ma says, dumping clothes into a washer. It's stuffed pretty tight. She pulls out a towel, then another, gives them a whiff and a shake, and throws them back into the basket, saying, "These can go another week."

As she pours detergent into the load, something catches her eye, and she reaches into the washer, pulls out my stained underwear, and asks, "This here yours?"

"No, Ma. It's Benny's."

"Benny got his period?"

"Yup. While he was at school. Lucky for him, his friend had a pad to spare."

"You all right, baby?"

I nod.

"Why didn't you say nothing?"

"'Cause there's nothing to say. I handled it."

Ma feeds the machine quarters, and water gushes out strong like a fire hose. She's doing that thing with her fingers she does when she's hankering for a smoke. She shuts the lid.

"Well, welcome aboard," she says, walking out of the laundry room.

I follow her out. She walks up the hill, sits down, and

pats a spot on the grass next to her, telling me to take a seat. I sit down.

"How's school?" Ma asks.

"I ran for president," I say, and lie down on the hill. Grass pricks at my back.

"No kidding," she says, lying back with me.

"I lost."

"That's too bad. President Mickey McDonald. It's got a nice ring, don't it?" she says, resting a wrist on her forehead.

"I was sad at first, but then I was like, 'Phew,' 'cause I made some promises I know I couldn't deliver."

"Like what?"

"I said if I'm president, I'd make sure everyone got plenty of food and friends and school supplies."

"Then good thing you lost. Nothing worse than broken promises."

"You mean like how Daddy done?"

If she had a cigarette, she'd be blowing a long stream of smoke at the orange sky and flicking ashes into the grass just about now. Instead, she rubs her eyes and runs her hands through her frizzy hair. Ma looks worn out. Last time I saw her looking fresh and pretty was when she and Daddy were getting ready for a funeral.

"Oh yeah," she says, and sighs.

We both look up at the sky. It's spacious and majestic.

Light flickers from some fireflies hanging on to summer. The machines in the laundry room rumble and tumble.

"Ma?"

"Mick?"

"You ever wish he'd come back?"

"Sometimes."

"Like when?"

"Like when I'm at work, sitting in that booth in the middle of the night, worrying if this lousy job's even going to last. They're automating these tolls, you know. Then I get to worrying about you and Benny. After all the worrying quiets down, it gets so darn lonely."

Ma starts to cry. A tear slides down the side of her face. With my thumb, I stop it from reaching her ear.

"You don't have to worry about me and Benny, Ma. I'm taking care of us," I say.

She sits up, wipes away tears, and says, "I'm sorry, Mickey. Oh, good Lord. You ever wonder how you end up somewhere? How in heavens did I get here? I need to find me another job. Wooo-weeee. All right. Enough of this," she says, fanning her face. "We got to look on the bright side. Bright side, where are you?"

"You got a job," I say.

"We got a roof," she says.

"We're soon going to have clean clothes."

"We got our fur babies."

"My butt don't get dunked in toilet water no more. You don't know how many times that happened when he was home," I say, sitting up.

"Good one. And even when he was here, he wasn't here," she says.

"His talk was too sweet to be true," I say.

"Left us with nothing but cavities."

"I didn't like when you two got to fighting. That was scary. I hated the D word. Divorce. Don't it sound like someone forcing you to divide yourself in half? Divorce. That's what it felt like, Ma. When y'all fought, it was like I was getting split in half. Like I was getting torn."

"Oh, Mick."

"But I don't know why I was so scared of the big D, 'cause the fighting happened when y'all were together. That's how it went. He'd come home. We'd all be happy for a minute. Then the fighting," I say.

"Unless he was sleeping."

"Daddy slept a lot."

"And I hated his snoring."

"It was so loud. He sounded like a tortured hippo."

"One time I thought it was Charlie howling."

"It'd wake me up in the middle of the night. But it was weird 'cause . . . I don't know . . . I kind of didn't mind it too much. I don't know . . . I guess it kind of made me feel safer when I heard his snoring," I say, my voice cracking.

I wipe my tears. Ma puts her arm around me. I lean into her. She says, "I guess I'm going to have to start snoring, then."

thirteen

Ok's postcard sits on a pile of junk mail on the couch. It's made from a Ritz cracker box. Took him long enough to write back. It says:

Hi President Yoo No Hoo,

Did you win? My new school is kind of like your knock-knock jokes—predictable yet unpredictable and funny yet not. Sometimes. I was going to complain about how hard my summer was, but yours sounds worse so I'm not even going to mention how scary and annoying new stuff can be. Things are different here. It's kind of fancy. I thought I liked fancy, but I'm not so sure anymore. But I do like Lassie, my new dog. He's actually the deacon's dog, but he's been following me around like he's mine or I'm his. He sleeps at the foot of my bed. Yeah, I still call him the deacon. Appa doesn't feel right. Not yet. Appa

is "dad" in Korean. FYI. Anyway, Chesterfield
who?

 From,
 Ok

I go to the kitchen and rummage through the cabi-
nets for boxes. Nothing catches my eye. I look in the
freezer. We got Ellio's frozen pizzas. I open the box,
empty it, and cut out a postcard. It's the perfect size. I
hurry to my room, shut the door, and write:

Chesterfield like a semi loser 'cause he lost the
election to Sydney Stevenson. I gave it my all. I
fell on my face, lost a tooth and swallowed it. It
was a canine, my last baby tooth, which is a total
phew 'cause I won't have a toothless grin for the
rest of my days, but as God is my witness, there
is indeed a black hole in my smile for now. Benny
says it looks like I got a black bean stuck in my
teeth. All my baby teeth are gone now. You know
what that means? I'm a grown-up. We should
swap 'cause I love fancy. Lassie sounds like the
sweetest thing. You think him and Charlie would
play nice? Before I forget, I got something urgent
to ask you. What do you know about chew-suck?
I need info on Chuseok ASAP. Like, what am I

supposed to wear? Write back fast. You take too long. You move slower than molasses on a snowy day.

    Your friend,
    Mickey

fourteen

I'm trying so hard to mind my manners that I'm sweating bullets underneath this potato sack of a sweater. The only reason I wore it was 'cause of the leaves embroidered in the colors of autumn, and Sun Joo said Chuseok is all about the autumn harvest. It's like Thanksgiving, but Korean-style.

There's a bunch of people here at Sun Joo's home, but not one of them is wearing anything with the autumn-harvest theme.

What I needed to mind was my socks. I had to take my shoes off. My socks look like rags, all covered in dog and cat hair. It's like I got a pair of ferrets for feet. They got holes, too. My big toes stick out like a pair of naked mole rats.

I follow Sun Joo in her apartment like the way she follows me around at school.

We walk past this big low table in the living room. Every inch of it is covered with food. And it ain't set up like a church potluck with Crock-Pots and casseroles and bags of chips. This food don't look like it's meant for eating. It's like the mannequin of food. It's too pretty to eat.

Not all of it is pretty. The pyramids of apples, oranges, and grapes are pretty. Even the watermelon with a flat top looks pretty. But the naked chicken with its butt sticking up? And a mound of what looks to me like brown worms? And the stack of crusty fish with eyes staring up at me? Not pretty. *What you looking at? I'll have you know I'm a guest here, so quit your fishy stares before I eat you up.*

The prettiest food of all is the mountain of glossy white, green, and pink candies shaped like baby crescent rolls at a corner of the table. I pull on Sun Joo's shirt and ask, "What's that?"

"This one? This is tteok," she says.

"You mean like 'lucky-duck quack-quack'?"

"No, not duck. Tteok. It's the rice cakes, but you're right, Mickey. Rice cake is lucky, so it's lucky tteok," she says.

"See? Lucky tteok. I like that."

"It's like the dessert. It's chewy and sweet inside."

"So is that why y'all call it chew-suck? 'Cause you chew and suck all this food?"

"No. That not right," she says, rolling her eyes and

shaking her head like she don't know what to do with me.

"I know. I know. I was just trying to be funny. That's the way I remember Korean. Like 'annyeonghaseyo'? I remember it 'cause it sounds like 'onion-hi-say-yo,'" I say.

"What floats boat," she says, which cracks me up.

"No. That not right," I say, imitating her.

"What float the boat?"

"Warmer."

"What floats a boat?"

"Warmer."

"I don't care. Is my boat. I float how I want."

"Whatever floats your boat."

"Congratulation! You got! Take you so long time!" she says, patting my head.

"Watch the hair."

Sun Joo's different here at her home. She walks with her back straight, hair off her face, and nose turned up like she rules all the little kids running around her place. She don't whisper like she does at school. Her voice got volume here. She got sass and snapitude.

She leads me to the kitchen, where a bunch of women are working their butts off, cooking at the stove, cleaning at the sink, deep-frying chicken wings on the floor, opening and closing the fridge. It bustles like the kitchen of a real restaurant. They talk and laugh and talk and click their tongues and laugh about I don't know what 'cause it's all in Korean, but it sounds and feels like family fun.

"Eomma," Sun Joo calls, zigzagging her way to the woman at the sink.

When the woman turns around to have a look at me, I get a look at her and flash back to the first day when she delivered Sun Joo to Ms. T's science class. That wasn't but a blink ago, but it feels like a bazillion years.

Sun Joo's ma takes off her dripping-wet rubber gloves and lets her daughter push her toward me. Sun Joo's talking Korean, but I hear my name except she says it like "me key."

"This is my Eomma," Sun Joo says.

"Onion-ha-say-yo," I say.

"Uh," Sun Joo's ma says, nodding.

"Did that come out right?"

"Uh, *annyeong*. Nice to meet you, Mi Ki. You are good friend to Sun Joo. She say you help very, very much at school," she says.

"Oh, I don't know about that. Sun Joo probably helps me more than I help her. She's gotten me out of some bad binds. I can get myself into some real messes. Like this one time during science lab, I had no clue—I mean like totally clueless about what we were supposed to be doing measuring the pH of this and the pH of that—and

I'm just like 'Can I eat this baked potato now; science ain't my thing,' and Sun Joo here took over like a real pro, and all because of her, we got an A on the lab. Don't know what I'd do without her. See this here? Fell on my face and lost a tooth last week. It's a baby canine, and don't ask me why they call it that 'cause it's not like a dog or anything. Imagine calling a dog a molar or something. Don't make any sense. Anyway, it's nice to meet you. How do you do?" I say.

"Mi Ki like the talking," her mom says.

"I do. I do like the talking. I can talk, talk, talk, talk, talk. My daddy says I got the gift of gab. I talk nonstop when he's home because he's hardly home, so when he is, I gotta catch him up on everything. I don't know, maybe I'm just nervous, but don't get me wrong, I ain't feeling nervous right now 'cause I'm too happy to be here celebrating chew-suck with y'all. By the way, thank you so much for inviting me. There ain't no better feeling in the world than getting included in a special family gathering 'cause it makes you feel like you're part of the family, and that's a good feeling, and all the food looks and smells so delicious, and I can't wait to try one of them tteoks on that beautiful spread you got out there. Tteok. Right? Did I say that—"

And before I can finish my question with "right," a grandma comes up to me and shoves food into my mouth, shutting me up. She puts her hand on my face and pets my cheek. Whatever she put in my mouth is yum-yum-yum. I want to say that I've had this before over at Ok's mom's wedding, and I know it's a dumpling and called mandu, which is an easy Korean word to remember for reasons I ain't going to get into 'cause I'm trying to mind my manners, if you know what I mean. Think about it. Man. Doo. Doo. So I keep my lips pressed together and chew.

The grandma looks up at me. She's only about as tall as Benny. Wrinkles cover her face, reminding me of how my palm looks when I close my hand after a spread of glue dries. Her permed hair sticks out frizzy and puffed like an Afro. The ends look purple in the kitchen light. Her silver roots look like a headband around her head. She's shaped round like a beanbag.

Sun Joo talks Korean to her, saying "me key" again.

"This is grandmother," Sun Joo says.

"Hi. Thank you for the mandu. That was yummy," I say.

Sun Joo translates. The grandma takes my hand and rubs it between hers, giggling and nodding at me. I don't know what to do, so I giggle and nod back.

"She say you are so plump and pretty."

"Really? Why, that's the nicest thing anyone's ever said to me. Thank you, Mrs. Sun Joo's grandma!"

"You can call Halmae," Sun Joo says.

"Howl-may? Did I say that right? Like howl-may-I-help-you if a dog was talking to a customer?"

"No. That not right, but warm enough."

"Thank you, Howl-may!"

Howl-may puts my face in her hands, looks into my eyes, and says something in Korean. Sun Joo talks Korean back to her, putting her arm around Howl-may.

"What'd she say? Did she say I look like Miss America?"

"She say you are angel."

"Oh my Lord of Lords! That's even better! Thank you, Howl-may! Thank you for them kind words! They really warm my heart and lift my spirits," I say, as Sun Joo starts pulling me out of the kitchen. "Wait. Wait. Don't Howl-may want to say more nice things to me?"

Sun Joo pulls me toward one of the bedrooms. She opens the door. Her room crawls with little kids, jumping on her bed, sitting at and on her desk, playing hide-'n'-seek in her closet, playing jacks with rocks on her floor.

"How in tarnation do you play jacks with rocks?"

Sun Joo shouts something in Korean, and they all gasp and go shooting out of the room. She shuts and locks her door. She plops down on her bed. I plop down next to her. Her bed squeaks.

"What in heavens is this thing made out of? Oh my Lord of Lords, please don't tell me it's baby minks, 'cause that would make me sadder than the mama mink who lost her poor babies to this divine blanket, but holy heckers, this feels so plush and soft. You ever feel something so soft you just want to die?"

"It made of polyester."

I burst out laughing. It ain't even that funny, but something about the way Sun Joo said it all serious and slow and soft revved up my giggles.

"One hundred percent."

I laugh louder.

"Machine wash."

"Stop!"

"Made in Korea."

"Stop! You going to make me pee! Stop!"

"This is *dam-yo. Dam-yo.* But you say wrong and you say like 'damn you.'"

I am losing it now. My stomach's cramping up. Tears running down my face. And I gotta cross my legs 'cause I'm going to wet my pants.

Then she puts her hand on my mouth to shut me up, saying, "Shhh! Shhh!"

"Stop! You going to make me pee!" I mumble into her palm.

"Listen."

89

It's quiet. It's like everyone in the other room left or something. I look around. Taped above her window is a poster of Jesus knocking on a door. Taped on her closet door is a poster of Jesus sitting with a bunch of kids. The window itself is covered with her own art. Sunlight shows through sheets of notebook paper painted with watercolors. Black birds flying over a rainbow. Stars twinkling in the night. A maple leaf glowing with the autumn colors of orange, yellow, red bleeding into one another. The last painting is the back of two girls holding hands and walking under a rainbow. The one girl looks like Sun Joo, and the other girl, as much as I hate to assume 'cause it makes an ass out of you and me, looks just like me, roller skates and big hair and all. I get up to have a closer look, point to the painting, and ask in a loud whisper, "Is that us?"

Sun Joo jumps out of bed, grabs my wrist, and pulls me out of the room. We walk into the living room. It's quiet. Everyone stands, looking at the table of food. Sun Joo pulls me toward the glass doors of the balcony and parks me there. She goes to stand next to her ma and grandma, who've changed their outfits, by the way. Oh my heavens! They got on these dresses that's putting me in a spell of longing. I stare at the bright colors. Pink. Red. Purple. Blue. Gold. They look like flowers. I drool.

I'm guessing this here's Sun Joo's daddy kneeling at the table of food. He strikes a match. He lights a stick on the small table, which is in front of the big table, which has all the food on it. He stands up, backs away, then bows to the food. This ain't no regular bow and curtsy. His face touches the floor. He bows again. Face to floor again. Good thing we ain't wearing shoes. He pours something into a cup and holds it to the smoke rising off the stick. He puts chopsticks on a plate and sticks a spoon into a bowl of rice. It's like he's having a tea party, but the mood ain't fun and giggles. It's serious. It feels like a funeral.

Then everyone takes turns bowing. Sun Joo bows. Then she stands next to the man who started the bowing. I was right. He's her daddy. He got his arm around her. She got her head tilting against his chest. Side by side, they look alike. He don't look like how he looked in Ms. T's class that first day. Sun Joo don't look how she looked. I guess this ain't school. People look different in different places. I wonder how I look right now.

I lean against the glass door. Outside the leaves blaze with autumn colors. Red. Yellow. Orange. It's like the trees are on fire. I see my reflection. I smile, give myself a little wave, and whisper, "Onion, Mi Ki. You going to be all right." My breath fogs the glass. I write "MSM was here" on the glass and draw a heart around it.

I smell smoke.

Sun Joo's daddy holds fire in his hand. It's a sheet of paper. He's burning it in front of everyone. I don't know why. Maybe it's like a magic show. He holds it and holds it and holds it, letting the paper burn till it can't burn no more without setting his hand on fire. He drops the flame into a metal bowl. Ashes float up. Waves of smoke move through the room. I hope the smoke detector don't go off.

Sun Joo comes over to me, and I ask her, "What's up with all that bowing and burning?"

"Ancestor stuff," she says, pulling open the glass door. She steps outside. I follow.

It's nice out here. Sun's about to set. I don't normally like fall 'cause of school starting and days getting shorter and everything dying and the air stinking like ratty old sneakers, but this feels all right.

Sun Joo shuts the door. She drags two cinder blocks from the corner of the balcony and sets them side by side near the railing. She sits on one, so I go over and sit on the other. People are getting food inside.

"So was that like calling on the dead? You know, like a séance?"

"Séance?"

"Yeah. I don't think there's any food at a séance. You don't really gotta feed the ghost, but you sit in a circle and the leader of the séance gets possessed by the ghost and the ghost talks through them. And you can ask the ghost questions like who killed you and who am I going to marry and what's the winning lottery number. Like Whoopi Goldberg in *Ghost*. You see that movie?"

"No."

"Same. I didn't see it either. I just heard about it."

"It's not séance. It's just for respecting ancestors," she says.

"Speaking of ghosts, what're you going to wear for Halloween?" I ask.

"Halloween? I don't know."

"I'm thinking about dressing up as Gidget. Like in the show? You ever watch that? I don't know, maybe put on one of them 1950s swimsuits? But I'd need a surfboard. Maybe I could make one out of cardboard. You know what you need to wear? One of them dresses."

"What dress?"

"One your ma and grandma have on."

"You mean *hanbok*?"

"How'd you say that?"

"*Hanbok*."

"Oh, that one's easy. Han as in Han Solo and bok as in Ok, my friend's name. You should wear a *hanbok* for Halloween. Is your ma going to let you borrow hers?"

"I have mine."

"You got your own *hanbok*? Why ain't you wearing it?"

"It's soooooo uncomfortable. It's too tight on here. I can't even breathe. It's worse than bra. It's sooooo itchy and make my neck feel like it's choking in a box and it's like a big umbrella and you can't walk or move or sit or breathe or talk because it's, like, choking you. I hate the *hanbok*," she says.

"I am telling you, Sun Joo. If you wear that thing for Halloween, you will win the costume contest. Hands down. People are going to be ooohing and ahhhing like you're some Korean princess. I money-back guarantee it. It's going to make you popular."

"Popular? You mean like Sydney? No, I don't believe it. Sydney is so pretty. She look like the supermodel."

"How much you want to bet?"

The glass door opens. Howl-may brings out two plates of food. She has towels tucked into her armpit. She says something in Korean to Sun Joo, and Sun Joo says something back. I stand up, take my plate, and say, "Thank you! This looks so delicious! I can't wait to eat it up. Thank you, Howl-may!"

"Uh-uh," she says, nodding. She says something to me in Korean. I ask Sun Joo what it means.

"She say to eat a lot."

Sun Joo takes her plate. Howl-may lays towels down next to the cinder blocks, saying something. It sounds like scolding. She's shaking her head like *tsk-tsk*. Then she goes back inside.

"What's that for?"

"She say girls should not sit on the cold things," Sun Joo says, putting her plate down on the cinder block.

"Why not?" I ask, following her lead.

"Because it's bad for the girl stuff," she says, sitting down on the towel.

"What girl stuff?" I ask, sitting down next to her.

"You don't know the girl stuff? The menseh. Because then we cannot have the babies."

"What? For real? Ewwwww. No thank you. I don't want no babies. Go get me a bag of ice to sit on."

"You are sooooo weird."

"You're so weird," I say, and bump my shoulder against hers.

"You are more weird," she says, and bumps me back.

"You are the queen of weird. You know why? I'll tell you why. 'Cause you got yourself this beautiful *hanbok* dress thing and you refuse to wear it. Shame, shame, shame. That's like hiding your shine. Don't you know that song? 'This little light of mine, I'm going to let it shine'? You got to stop hiding your shine. What would your ancestors think?"

"I don't care what ancestors think. They are dead," she says, and bites into a dumpling.

I snort out laughing, spitting out bits of spinach. I say, "Sun Joo Moon, you are so shiny."

"Only sometimes."

"I bring it out in you, don't I?"

"You don't," she says, shaking her head, her mouth full of food.

"You know I do. Admit it."

"Maybe little bit."

"I got you a nickname. I'm calling you Sunny from now on."

"Sunny? You mean like sun in solar system? It's so bright it make you hot and sweat all the time and make the skin burn up and wrinkly. My mom say sun is sooooo bad for the skin and eyes because it make you blind if you look at too long not wearing the sunglasses. It's just big ball burning up with the fire. It's like ten thousand degrees. You come too close, you burn. Oh, I like. Okay! Call me Sunny. Sunny Moon."

"Girl, you crack me up."

"How about I call you the McDonald?"

"How about I call you the Moon-butt?"

Sun Joo chuckles as she slurps up glassy noodles. I slurp up mine.

I poke my chopsticks into a tteok. I sniff. I put the plump pink rice cake into my mouth, bite down and chew.

"It don't taste like I thought it would. It don't taste like nothing. That ain't chocolate in there, is it?"

"No. It's bean."

"Beans for dessert? That's, like, false advertising. Imagine biting into a Twinkie and getting cottage cheese. What's your favorite candy?"

"Ummm. It's the Hershey's Kisses. It shape like *ddong*."

"*Ddong?*"

"Is the poo-poo in Korean."

I laugh so loud some heads inside turn to check us out. It's getting dark out here, so I can see pretty good what's going on inside. People are starting to leave. Howl-may looks like she's giggling up a storm, saying good-bye to everyone.

"You wear the bracelet?"

"Right here," I say, and show it to her.

"I have too," she says, and shows hers to me.

We bump our wrists together like the Wonder Twins, then go back to eating. I feel honest-to-angels happy inside right here, right now, eating all this good food, sitting with my best friend, Sunny Moon.

fifteen

I step off the bus and walk toward the school, Ma's blue bathrobe covering my Gidget bathing suit costume and Ma's ironing board tucked under my arm like it's for surfing.

I head over to my locker, scanning the hall for signs of Sunny. She said she wasn't going to wear a costume, so I keep an eye out for her usual cardigan sweater, baggy jeans, white sneakers, and the top of her bowed head. I can't tell who's who in the hall because everyone's dressed up as someone else. There goes Dorothy from *The Wizard of Oz*. No place like home. Frankenstein. Jason. Wonder Woman. A red M&M. A yellow M&M. A blue M&M. I love group costumes. Last year, some teachers dressed as beatniks. Black turtlenecks, black pants, black berets. I didn't even know what a beatnik was. I thought they were ninjas. They looked so cool, like they were a secret society. Made me curious enough to look it up. Beatniks were writers from the fifties who got so fed up that they did a bunch of cussing and drugging and having sex and hitting the road. Halloween is so educational. The books were kind of boring to me, but I do recall feeling struck by a line that went something like, "There was nowhere to go but everywhere, so just keep on trucking under the stars." Reminded me of Daddy.

"Boo."

"Oh, hi, Larry. I mean Law," I say, turning my lock.

"You can call me Larry. Law didn't really stick."

"Nice costume. I like the earring. How'd you make that?"

"My mom's really into canning. These bands are all over the house."

"How'd you get that on your ear?" I ask, opening my locker.

"See?" Larry says, taking off his bandanna. The jar lid band is sewn on the scarf.

"Cool! So what are you?"

"I was going for pirate."

"You need an eye patch."

"Aaarrrgh. I knew I forgot something."

I take off my robe, hang it on the hook, and put on my sunglasses. I put on lipstick, spray my hair, check my pigtails in the mirror, and shut my locker. With fist on hip and ironing board tucked under my arm, I say, "Surf's up."

"You know, I have a Hawaiian shirt. I could've been Frankie," he says.

"I'm not Annette. I'm Gidget," I say, walking away from him. I see Sydney Stevenson at the end of the hall. Her costume looks really cute.

"Gidget's got a boyfriend, doesn't she?" Larry says, following me.

"So?" I say, walking faster.

My board accidentally whacks him.

"Ouch," he says.

"That's what you get for standing so close, Moon-doggie," I say, holding the board above my head and making my way through the hall.

"What was that?"

I need to find Sunny. Still no sign of her in the hall. I'm getting worried. It's crazy out here. If you don't know Halloween, this could freak you out. I hope she's not crying under the stairs.

Sydney stands at the end of the hall talking to her girls. High ponytail. Pencil tucked behind ear. Fifties-inspired pink waitress dress. Polka-dot hankie around her neck. White apron trimmed in ruffles. I'll bet she's got on a "Sydney" name tag. She stands taller than usual. It's like she grew three inches. As I get closer, I check out her footwear. Roller skates. She's got on my red, white, and blue roller skates. They're not mine, but they look just like mine. We got the same taste. And I feel a mess of pride and excitement. What a coinkydink!

I stand behind her, trying not to breathe too heavy, hoping she'll turn around and notice me. She doesn't, so I tap her arm. She peeks over her shoulder. She barely turns her head, but her ponytail swings.

"Hey, I'd like a cheeseburger, fries, and a strawberry milkshake. Sydney, you and I, we're the same decade! Ain't that a hoot? You, working at the drive-in. Me, catching waves at the beach. And I got those same skates! They don't fit me no more, but I still love them. You remember that speech I gave during elections? Or maybe you remember last year's talent show? Remember that?"

Up and down and up again her eyes go. Her long lashes remind me of the prongs of a pitchfork. If looks could kill, I just got stabbed to death. I shut up. I normally don't let other people's meanness make me feel small, but Sydney shrank me down to a microscopic vacuole.

She turns her back to me and says something to her circle of friends. They laugh. I really ought to just walk away, but I stand there paralyzed with humiliation and longing. I want in so bad. I check out the other girls one by one. What's so great about them? Boring costumes. Obviously store bought. No one sparkles.

Then I catch a glimpse of this yellow princess ball gown on Sydney's other side. The dress is big, like Scarlett O'Hara big. The color glows like the promises of the yellow brick road. Starting at the hem, my eyes go up, following a satiny rainbow sash up the middle, and I'm feeling déjà vu 'cause I know the shape of this dress. The rainbow sash ends with a bow over the girl's heart. The sleeves are rainbow too. They look like a pair of rainbow wings. I know this girl.

"Is that you, Sun Joo Moon?" I say, pushing Sydney out of my way.

Sun Joo smiles and waves at me. She's doing the Miss America wave. Her hair is tied up into a ballerina bun, and she's wearing makeup. Her head is held high. I can't believe it! I feel so proud of her!

"Didn't I tell you? Didn't I? You look amazing in your . . . What's it called again? Han-as-in-Han-Solo-bok-as-in-Ok dress! Oh my tarnation! Look at you! Ladies, listen up! This here is a *hanbok*. Say it with me. Han as in Han Solo. Han . . ."

I'm waiting for them to say "han," but they all stare at me blank, like I'm a heap of nothing. Then their eyes roll back like they're about to faint and topple over like dominoes.

"Like in *Star Wars*? The movie? A long time ago in a galaxy far, far away?"

Eyes keep rolling.

"You don't know *Star Wars*?"

"Excuse you," Sydney says, yanking at my board. I lose my grip, and my surfboard goes tumbling onto the floor, the legs clanking out. Reminds me of that commercial. *Help! I've fallen and I can't get up!*

The bell rings. Sydney grabs Sun Joo's wrist. As she pulls her away from me, she says, "Her name is Sunny."

"I know! I gave her that name!"

"Go put on some clothes," Sydney says, rolling away with my best friend.

There they go.

"Don't you dare. Don't you dare go following them like some poor stray. Don't you dare. Stand firm. Stand straight. Chin up. Hold your ground," I tell myself, forcing my fists onto my hips. I'm shaking a little from feeling sad and mad. I'm panting. I'm trying to take a deep breath, but Ma's old girdle and bra fit stiff and tight like casts. Can't fill up with enough air. The crusty pink spray paint makes me itch. The cotton balls I glued on for trim starts to tickle. I breathe out. I crack a smile. I look down at my ironing board all sprawled out in the hall, pretending to be something it's not. Poor thing wants to be riding ocean waves instead of taking the heat of an iron. I pick it up, tuck the rusty legs in, and carry it to homeroom.

sixteen

Sunny and I sit at our usual lunch spot at the table in the back of the cafeteria. She pulls at the collar of her *hanbok*, scratches her shoulder, and opens her lunch box. I dig into my hot lunch. Spaghetti and one meatball. I pierce my spork into the meatball, hold it up, and say, "See? This here's a gogi ball. Right?"

I'm about to ask Sunny about going trick-or-treating with me, but she's too busy staring over my shoulder and pointing at herself and smiling while looking confused and shaking her head. It's like she's saying, "Me? Who me?" I turn around to see what's going on. Sydney and her girls are waving at Sunny.

"They want you to come over," I say, shaking my chocolate milk.

"Me?" Sunny asks, waving back.

"Yes, you. Sure as heck ain't me they're waving at," I say.

"Why?"

"'Cause they like you now. 'Cause they like your costume. What'd I tell you?" I say, and drink my milk.

"Oh no."

"What?"

"They coming this way."

I turn around, and sure enough, Sydney's two best friends are walking over to us. Nawsia and Tammy. It's weird seeing them without Sydney in the middle. It's like two slices of bread with nothing in between. It's a nothing sandwich. Sunny closes her lunch box like she's hiding her food.

"Hi, Sunny," they singsong in unison.

"Hi," Sunny says.

"Hey there! So what brings you to this neck of the woods?" I say, slurping up noodles.

Nawsia looks down at my hot lunch and says, "I'm sorry, but is that, like, any good? It just looks so unappetizing. What're those black dots?"

I chew as fast as I can so I can tell her it's not that bad, but I can't chew and swallow faster than I talk, so I talk with food in my mouth and end up spitting out spaghetti bits, which makes Tammy and Nawsia frown like I'm throwing up on them and turn their backs to me.

"Sydney wants to ask you something," Nawsia says to Sunny.

"Come over to our table," Tammy says.

"Your dress is so pretty."

"Sydney wants you to come over."

"She thinks you're, like, so cute."

"Thank you," Sunny says.

"She wants to ask you something," Nawsia says.

"Okay," Sunny says.

"Well? Are you coming?" Tammy asks, tapping her nails on the table.

"Okay. I go. One minute. I go in one minute," Sunny says, holding up one finger.

"Well, don't keep her waiting," Nawsia says.

"She might change her mind just like that," Tammy says, snapping her fingers.

The two walk away, returning to their table to report back to Sydney.

"What Sydney want?" Sunny whispers to me.

"Only one way to find out," I say.

"I don't want to go," Sunny says, pulling at her collar.

There's a big part of me that wants to tell her to forget about them. If she don't want to go, she don't have to go. Leave Sydney waiting. Stand Sydney up. No big deal. Be that girl who blew Sydney off. Sunny can stay right here with me 'cause we have each other. We're best friends.

But there's another part of me that knows this

here's an opportunity of a lifetime for little Miss Sunny Moon (and maybe me, too). She's going to be popular (and maybe me, too). I can't let this chance pass us by.

"Listen up, Sunny. The one and only Sydney Stevenson, president and captain of step and most popping popular girl, wants to talk to you. That's like being summoned by the queen. You gotta get yourself over there. I know if I was in your shoes, I would've been there, like, yesterday. Get. Go. Run along," I say, shooing her like Ma does to me and Benny.

"I don't know," she says, lowering her head.

"What'd I tell you? Chin up!" I say, slapping the table.

"Okay," Sunny says, and eyes the three girls, slowly pulling herself up.

"That's my girl. Time to shine. If you need me, tap your nose with your pinkie like this, and I'll swoop in for a rescue. Okay?"

"That look like picking booger."

"Fine, then pull at your ear like this. Okay?"

"Okay. Wish me the good luck," she says, and walks over to Sydney's table.

"Lucky duck," I say, and watch her move across the cafeteria. That dress makes Sunny look like she's gliding across the floor like some remote-control windup princess doll on wheels.

seventeen

If I could have any superpower right now, it'd be invisibility, which is nuts since being seen is what I live for. But if I were invisible, I could be over there with Sunny and Sydney and Nawsia and Tammy and hear what they're saying to her.

Sydney puts her arm around Sunny, saying something into her ear. Nawsia and Tammy huddle in, bobbing their heads like a pair of pigeons. They touch Sunny's *hanbok* sleeves. I keep an eye on Sunny's hands to see if they're going up to her ears for a tug, tug, but nothing. She keeps them down by her sides. Sydney moves the entire huddle out of the cafeteria. There they go.

What do I do?

A part of me wants to follow them and get in on all the action, but I stay put. A year ago I would've chased them down, gotten to the bottom of this, and called dibs on Sunny, but something about me this year—I don't know what it is, call it second-guessing, call it being mature, call it pussyfooting. Maybe it's 'cause I got my period and the hormones and all. Maybe I'm all messed up in the heart 'cause Daddy left. I don't know. But I ain't feeling like my old self 'cause my old self would not hear of staying put like a bump on a log all paralyzed, chewing lettuce soggy with Thousand Island dressing, thinking all these thoughts, sitting by as they steal my friend away, and feeling all mixed up inside. Boy, oh boy, are my feelings all in a tangle. I'm excited for Sunny. I honest-to-angels am. I'm happy for her. I'm also nervous like I'm about to drop down a coaster ride. I'm nervous like my name ain't going to be called as the winner of the pageant. I'm worried like I'm about to lose something I love. I feel sorry like I regret being so pushy. I feel jealous. I feel sad. I feel left out. I feel left behind.

I bite into the garlic bread. It's like a gigantic crouton with a yellow stain on it. Crumbs fall all over my stupid Gidget costume. I suddenly want to cover up. I want Ma's robe, but it's in my locker, and there's chocolate pudding for dessert. I peel open the lid and squeeze the container until a glob of pudding rises and bubbles. I slurp it up just like I did way back when Sunny and me were first getting to be friends. I miss her.

In strut the four of them through the cafeteria doors like they're walking up a runway. Sydney, Tammy,

Nawsia, and Sunny. Except something's not right. That's not Sydney. That's not Sunny. Their heads got switched.

Sunny hurries over to me wearing a fifties waitress costume with Sydney's name tag. She's all smiles and giggles. She says, "Look, Mickey. We do swap. See? Swap."

"Why'd you let her do that?" I ask, feeling irritated.

"Because I hate wearing the *hanbok*. Is so itching me. This one feel better," she says, and twirls around like I don't know what her backside might look like.

"Well, you ain't winning no contest with that getup. You can kiss that dream good-bye."

"Is okay."

"Well, what else? What else did Sydney say? What else did y'all talk about?"

"She talk about the trick-or-treat."

"What about it?"

"She say to come with her."

"Oh. Did she?"

"Sydney is nice," Sunny says.

"So you're trick-or-treating with them?"

"I say okay because I thinking what Mickey do? What Mickey say? Mickey say okay. Mickey say get and go and good chance like that," she says, and shrugs.

"Oh, that's great. That's just great. You done great. You're going to have such a great time."

"I think so."

"You're going to tell me all about it, right? You're going to give me the scoopity scoop?"

"Yes, I tell you everything. But you come too, Mickey. You can come with us," she says.

"Did Sydney invite me too?" I ask, my eyes popping wide and my hopes rising like a slice of baloney in a frying pan.

"No, she don't say that, but I go ask. Sydney is nice. I ask if you can come too. We go together to trick-or-treating," she says, putting on her backpack. The waitress costume fits too big on her.

"Nah. Never mind. It's fine. I got plans anyway. Family stuff. You know," I say.

"Oh. Okay. Mickey? What is it? What is the trick-or-treat?" she asks.

"You don't know what trick-or-treating is?"

"I don't know."

I start laughing, but I stop as soon as I see Sunny's face go sad, and I say, "I'm sorry. I'm sorry. I didn't mean to laugh at you. So trick-or-treating is when kids get dressed up in costumes, go knocking on doors in their neighborhoods, and say 'trick or treat' to get candy."

"You go to friend's house?"

"You go to anyone's house. Friends, strangers, neighbors. Anyone. Everyone, if you can. The more you knock, the more candy you get."

"And everybody give the candy?"

"Yep."

"Is free?"

"Yep."

"That's so nice."

"It's a lot of fun. It's my favorite holiday. I bring back loads of candy. But make sure your bag is strong so it don't break. I lost a ton of candy one year 'cause my plastic had a hole in it," I say, picking up my tray. I throw away my trash.

When I get back to the table, the Sydney sandwich rolls along the aisle. Tammy and Nawsia are pulling Sydney along in her roller skates. I have to admit, the *hanbok* looks really pretty on her, but I want to rip it off and put it back on Sunny, where it belongs.

Sunny waits for me to get my things together. I look under the table. I look on the seats. I look on top of the table. I look under the table again. I scan the cafeteria. Where'd it go? Where'd my surfboard go? Who took Ma's ironing board?

eighteen

Once the dismissal bell rings, I hurry to the lost-and-found closet in the main office to see if Ma's ironing board showed up. Nothing. Then I run to the cafeteria for another look. I ask the janitor who's sweeping the floor if he's seen an ironing board. Nope. Then I retrace my steps, going back to each of my classrooms. The halls empty out as everyone leaves to head home. No ironing board. I run over to the auditorium. There's trash on the stage left from the costume contest, which Sydney won on account of Sunny's *hanbok,* which I think is plain wrong, wrong, wrong. I check bathrooms. Nothing. I give up and dash outside to be greeted with an emptying parking lot, cars turning onto the street. Not a yellow school bus in sight. I missed my bus.

I dash back into the main office to call home.

"May I?" I ask Ms. Bierman, pointing to her phone.

"Did you miss your bus, sweetie?"

"Yes, ma'am," I say, nearly choking back tears.

She turns the phone and hands me the receiver.

"Thank you," I say, and dial.

Busy tone. Ma's sleeping with the phone off the hook. I hang up and try again. Beep. Beep. Beep. I try again and again and again until Ms. Bierman asks, "Are you all right, baby?"

"Yes, ma'am," I say, returning the phone to her.

Mr. Graves, the vice principal, steps out of his office wearing a clown wig and a clown nose. He locks up and shakes his keys, telling everyone to make it a happy and safe Halloween.

"Get home for those trick-or-treaters!" he says before stepping into the hall.

I don't know why I do this, but I quietly follow Mr. Graves like I'm some stalker. I think I'm hoping he might give me a ride home. We get outside. He heads over to his car, pulling off his clown wig. He tucks it under his arm. Keeping my distance, I tiptoe follow him, trying to figure out how to word what I need. *May I please have a ride home?* I know this ain't normal, but are vice principals allowed to give us kids a ride home? I missed my bus. I need to get home. To trick-or-treat tonight. I got three cats and a dog. They need me. Our phone's off the hook. Ma's asleep. She's putting in overtime 'cause this here's her last week at the toll. She got laid off. They don't need her no more. Robot's taking her job. Daddy ain't coming back home. My little brother. I don't know if he's wearing a key today.

By the time I get some proper words strung together, Mr. Graves is backing out of his parking space and driving off to get ready for the trick-or-treaters.

It gets real quiet out here. I hear birds and distant traffic. I walk across the parking lot like I have somewhere to go, trying to breathe steady, trying not to freak into a panic.

As I pass the dumpster, I see the legs of my ironing board sticking out of the side opening. *There you are.* I run over and pull it out.

The cover's got TRASH written on it in black marker. I hope to Jesus that's not permanent, 'cause Ma's going to want answers, but then again, she ain't ironed anything for eons. Daddy was the last one to use it to press his one good dress shirt for his aunt Lynelle's funeral, which is how that stain got burned on there. Looks like the tip of a rocket ship. Three, two, one. Blast off.

As I fold the rusty legs, tears drip out of my eyes. I wouldn't call it crying 'cause I'm not making sad faces or pitiful sounds, but it's just water falling out of my eyes like if you get a cut, the blood leaks automatic. It's just nature doing her thing.

I wipe my cheeks, strap on my backpack, tuck the ironing board under my arm, and walk away from the school toward the traffic. Surf's up.

nineteen

I'm walking home. Can't be that far. I know the way.

Every street I cross, I switch arms. The ironing board weighs a ton.

I pass Wish Wash Laundromat, King's Pawnshop, Grande Market, and Pizza Oven. I stop for a second in front of Pizza Oven 'cause it smells good. A ghost cutout hangs on the window announcing their Halloween specials.

Do I believe in ghosts? Why, yes I do, thank you.

Ever since Daddy told us about how he never believed in ghosts, not even as a kid, but then his aunt Lynelle died and left him her old Monte Carlo, I have been a certified believer. She loved that car. He'd be driving it along, minding his business, when out of the blue he smelled her perfume. Bird of Paradise by Avon. He smelled it so strong it was like she was sitting right next to him, better yet, like she was sitting on him, better yet, like she was trying to possess him. He'd open the windows to air out the car, but to no avail. The whole thing reeked of Aunt Lynelle.

Then there was the incident with the radio station. Daddy likes country music just fine, but that's not what he listens to when he's driving. He listens to talk, and that's where his radio's fixed at. But this one time, he started the Monte Carlo, and the station was WMZQ. You guessed it. Aunt Lynelle's first pick. It was playing a song about tomorrow never coming. Daddy said he sold the Monte 'cause we needed the cash, but I think it was 'cause of the haunting.

Then Ma told the story about how when her Ma and Daddy died in that barn fire. Their porch swing would swing at the very hour they would've been out there swinging if they hadn't died. For ten whole minutes. Back and forth. Squeak and all. They took the swing down. But the very next day, there it was hanging on the porch again, swinging. "And guess who was sitting on it?" Ma asked in a spooky whisper.

Benny and I whimpered, "Who?"

"YOU!" she boomed.

We screamed our heads off.

When Ma and Daddy told us those ghost stories, it was one of the best days of my life. I was eight years old. We'd gotten back from trick-or-treating. Candy loot was sorted, exchanged, and organized accordingly.

Benny and I were tucked in bed. Charlie and the angels lounged with us. With Daddy on my bed and Ma on Benny's, the family ghost stories were shared. It beat Christmas morning. Never felt so close. Nothing like a good scare to bring a family together.

A car honks. Ma would flip the bird. It's like a reflex with her when she's driving. It's so embarrassing. Makes me want to open the car window and say I'm sorry.

Suddenly, moving headlights decorate the street. My feet hurt. My back aches. My arms feel sore. The sun's going down.

I walk toward Golden Gardens Assisted Living, which looks like a nice hotel building. Warm orange light glows out of their front windows and doors. The chairs in the lobby look plush and comfy. No one's sitting on them. I see a tray of cookies on the coffee table. There's a bowl of Halloween candy at the front desk. I bet they'd let me use their phone.

twenty

The doors of Golden Gardens open automatic.

"I'm sorry, but I don't know what's going on. Amanda quit this morning," says the receptionist. She's talking to an old woman wearing a pink feather boa and holding a Mardi Gras mask over her eyes.

Elevator music's playing in the lobby. It's coming from the boom box behind the front desk. The place smells like pine trees and pumpkin pie. I help myself to a sugar cookie shaped like a ghost.

"What are we to do about our masquerade?" the old woman asks.

"I'm sorry. I think it's canceled. Amanda was in charge of all that."

"Well, how about you, dear? Can't you do it?"

"That's not my job."

"I don't see why you can't be a good sport about it and get this shindig started. Look at me. I got all dressed up for it. I have my dancing shoes on," she says, waving her mask like a magic wand. Her hair glows white.

"I'm sorry. I have to stay here at the front desk and answer the phone and . . ." The receptionist looks over at me like she needs a rescue.

"Hi there!" I pipe in.

"Hi. What brings you to Golden Gardens? How can I help you?" the receptionist asks. Her name tag says "Claudia."

"May I please use your phone?"

"Are you here for the masquerade, darling?" the old woman says. "Well, it's been canceled. They put a stop to it because of that lazy Amanda. She was no good at her job. No good at all. She was supposed to be our events coordinator, but what events? I don't recall any events unless you're referring to those dreadful outings to Kmart."

"Here," Claudia says, giving me the phone.

As I dial, an old man dressed as Superman comes into the lobby with a walker and says, "Where this party at?" On his head is a glossy black toupee.

Our phone rings.

"Hello?" Benny answers.

"Put Ma on," I say.

"Where are you? Why ain't you here?"

"Get Ma."

121

"Maaaaaa!" Benny yells into the phone.

"Mickey, where in tarnation are you?" Ma says.

"I'm at that Golden Gardens place on East–West. You know. I'm fine. It's just I missed my bus. I'm sorry, Ma. I called, like, a million times, but our phone was busy. Did you have it off the hook? I've been walking this whole time."

"Worried sick, Mick. I've been worried sick."

"You can't keep the phone off no more. You know how annoying that busy tone gets? Beep. Beep. Beep. That's like being in hell. Busy tone for eternity. Can't get a call through. Can you come get me?"

"I'm late for work."

"Please, Ma. I'm going to miss a good chunk of trick-or-treating at this rate. Please. Pretty please? I'm butt-tired and hungry," I say.

"You think whining and begging's going to get you anywhere?"

I take a deep breath, change my tone, and say, "First, you hate that job. Second, this here's, like, your last week. Third, they laid you off. Don't you think you owe them and yourself one tardy?"

Ma takes a breath and says, "Oh, all right, fine. But don't go wandering off nowhere, 'cause if you ain't there, I'm going straight to work. You hear? I'm not looking for you," she says, trying not to sound proud of me. I can hear it in her voice. I can hear the smile she's trying to hide.

"Got it. I'm staying put. Right here in this lobby. One quick thing, Ma. Can you bring my dance CD?"

"Your what?"

"My dance CD with all the dance songs on it. You know the one. It's in the player."

"What for?"

"I got an idea. Please and thank you," I say.

"Fine," she says, and hangs up.

I hang up and wait to thank Claudia 'cause she's busy trying to quiet down the old folks. They're now up to five, six, seven. Mardi Gras–mask woman, Superman, tuxedo man, cat woman, Little Red Riding Hood, top-hat man, bunny woman. Then a few more old folks show up dressed like old folks. They want answers. They want the manager.

"Jerry's about to leave," Claudia explains.

"Over my dead—"

"You can't go in there," Claudia interrupts.

"Watch me."

"Okay. Fine. Just wait here. I'll get Jerry," Claudia says, and leaves the front desk.

"Doesn't that figure."

"No one cares anymore."

"It's not like it used to be."

"We deserve to have some fun around here."

"I've been waiting all day for this."

"I like your whiskers, Pauline."

"These took me hours. My hand was so shaky."

"Whatever happened to movie night?"

"That Amanda didn't know what she was doing."

"I wanted to dance tonight."

"I was all set."

"Nothing like a good dance to lift the spirits."

I can't stand it no more. I take Ma's robe off, clap my hands real loud, and blurt out, "Did someone say dance? Do y'all want to dance? Hi there, Golden Gardens! My name's Mickey! This here's my Gidget costume, and I'm going to teach y'all how to dance the Electric Slide! Y'all ready to do this? Everyone line up right here!"

"I know this dance."

"Did she say she's Gidget?"

"They did this one at my granddaughter's wedding."

"Can y'all see me? Let's start nice and easy. Watch me first. This here's the grapevine to the right, touch, then grapevine to the left, touch. Here I go again. Got that? Now follow along. I'm going to do it real slow. Right. Left step back. Right. Touch. Left. Right step back. Left. Touch. You got it! Let's do it again," I say.

We practice three more times. Everyone's doing it, even Superman back there with the walker.

"Let's move on. Watch me first. Grapevine right,

touch. Grapevine left, touch. Walk back for three and touch. See that? Let's add the walk back for three and touch. Come on. From the top," I say.

"Y'all are fast. Now, from here, step up, touch, step back, touch. Got that? Okay, from the top. Yes! This here's the tricky part, so watch. You're going to do a step scuff turn. See that? Step scuff turn. Do it with me."

"From the top!" someone shouts out.

We all Electric Slide, calling out the steps together. Grapevine right, touch. I'm having such a time. Some of them already know the dance and are helping the others out. We do it again and again until everyone's got it down. And like clockwork, Ma's car shows up at the front, and I tell them to keep going and excuse myself and run outside and grab my CD while Ma yells at me to come back here right now. I dash back into Golden Gardens and pop the CD into Claudia's boom box and turn up the volume and push play.

"It's electric!" I call out.

The music comes on. We all start dancing. We're doing the steps together. I hear a woo-hoo from the back. This here feels so good I'm cartwheeling inside. It's at the first step scuff turn that I see a man with a briefcase heading into the lobby. I'll bet that's Jerry the manager. He stops and watches us, nodding along to the music.

At the next grapevine right, touch, I see Ma marching up to the doors. She looks crabby. I keep on dancing. She walks into the lobby, stops by the comfy chairs, and crosses her arms. She watches us dance. She's tapping her foot, but I can't tell if it's 'cause she's peeved or if it's 'cause of the music. She walks over to me. I think she might grab my arm and drag me out to the car, so I dance like this here's my last dance, but she don't touch me. Instead, Ma gets next to me and joins us, grapevining to the left, touch, grapevining to the right, touch. We Electric Slide together for three whole rounds, and it's like something dreamy to see Ma dance, shimmying her shoulders and snapping her fingers and smiling like she don't got a care in the world.

I leave my CD to keep on playing, while Ma and me walk out of Golden Gardens.

As Ma drives us away, I watch them, all costumed up, moving together in the orange light to the Electric Slide, and I tell Ma all about Amanda and how she up and left her job as events coordinator just like that and how that was Jerry the manager watching us dance and how Golden Gardens needs someone real bad.

twenty-one

When I get home, Charlie wags his tail so hard he could boomerang a kid to the moon. He's so dizzy happy to see me, he's actually smiling, teeth and all. You ever see a dog smile? It's the best thing ever. Right up there with Reddi-Wip, wild applause, and trick-or-treating. He's begging me to take him with us. He's been cooped up all day with Sabrina, who's been in a mood lately. I know I shouldn't, but I tie a bandanna around Charlie's neck so he could pass for a farm dog and decide to bring him along.

Benny fussed, but I put him in an old pageant dress of mine. I put a little makeup on him, teased and sprayed his hair, and fastened onto his head the tiara I won at the Little Miss Darlin' Pageant in the category of Personal Expression. He whined, but what choice did he have? Dress up and free candy, or stay home and no candy.

Benny looks like a pageant gone bad, swinging his

candy bag and strutting his stuff out the door. He makes me laugh so hard my stomach stops grumbling.

Our first knock-knock is our neighbors. "Trick or treat," we say. Charlie barks.

"Is that you, Benny? I remember you when you were itty-bitty. Don't you look so adorable?" the woman says, like Benny's a newborn. She doesn't even acknowledge my existence. She puts Mary Janes in our bags. We say thank you and move on.

As we walk up the stairs to the next set of doors, Benny says, "I hate Mary Janes."

"Me too. But . . ."

"I know. I know. Beggars can't be choosers," he says, knocking on the next door.

"Don't tell that to Ma. You know what she'd say," I say.

"What'd I say about begging?" Benny says in Ma's voice.

"This ain't exactly begging, and I was going to say candy is candy is candy," I say.

"Mary Janes are yuck."

What's yuckier than Mary Janes? Bit-O-Honeys, circus peanuts, pencils, pennies, loose raisins, old Valentine chalk hearts, and candy corn that's not even in wrapping. Our building is giving out the worst candy ever.

As we run over to the next building, some kids on their way out tell us not to bother. The one apartment with candy is giving out old broken-up candy canes from Christmas.

"But I like candy canes," says Benny.

"You know where we should go for the real good candy? I'm talking about the big chocolate bars, like Snickers and Butterfingers and Kit Kats, and not the itty-bitty sizes they got the nerve to call fun. I'm talking about regular-size bars, the stuff you can grip like a handle and rip off with your teeth," I say, pulling him and Charlie toward the creek.

"They got Milky Ways?"

"I'll bet they do. We got to cross Route 12."

"Where the big houses are at?"

"Yeah, where the rich folks live."

"Big house means big candy?"

"Come on, Benny. Let's go!" I say, breaking into a jog.

twenty-two

A real nice lady dressed up as a witch gives me and
Benny extra plastic bags for double-plying 'cause
ours are about to bust since they're bulging with candy.
Real candy. Good candy. I'm talking Twix, Almond Joy,
Snickers, Milky Way, Hershey's, Reese's. You name it,
this place is dishing it out. It's like one big trick-or-
treating party. Kids crawling all over. Porch lights on.
Candles burning inside jack-o'-lanterns made from
pumpkins—I mean real pumpkins. One pumpkin was
carved to make it look like it was sick and throwing
up its innards, a bunch of seeds tangled up in a slimy,
stringy mess. Orange lights strung along railings
blinking and winking, making me want to wink back.
Glow-in-the-dark skeletons hanging from trees. One
house has a coffin that opens and laughs when you
walk up to it. One yard's a cemetery with a machine
blowing fog all over the tombstones. One yard's covered
in Halloween blowups with "Monster Mash" playing

through loudspeakers. One house left a cauldron of candy sitting there on the porch for all to take 'cause they couldn't be home to give it out. This whole place is in on it, making Halloween dreams come true. Even the cops. They blocked off the streets with their cop cars, lights flashing, so no one would get run over. It's Halloween heaven on this side of Route 12.

Lord knows I don't want this night to end, but it's getting late and Charlie's tongue's hanging out like he's dying of thirst and he's sitting down every chance he gets and we got ourselves enough candy to last us the entire year even with us sneaking bites between houses, so I tell Benny this here's our last knock.

"Nooooooo," he whines through lips red from a Blow Pop. He stomps. Smears of chocolate on his cheeks look like war paint. He yawns, sticking out his tongue, which looks bruised, all purplish brown, from eating all the colors brought to you by Skittles.

"Are you telling me we need to go home right here, right now?"

"No," he says, pulls out a Twizzler from his bag, sticks it into his mouth, wrapper and all, and chews.

We walk past a witch on a broomstick, hanging from a tree branch. Her face glows green. An orange and black wreath made of feathers hangs on the front door. In the middle of the hole shines the golden head of a lion. The feathers look like his mane. I lift the ring held between his teeth and drop it against the door. Knock-knock.

The door opens. A man wearing a Redskins football helmet and jersey looks down at us, holding a bowl of candy.

"Trick or treat," I say.

I elbow Benny.

"You said not to talk with my mouth full," he says, spraying bits of Twizzler and plastic.

"Hello. Hello. Hello-ween," the man sings out like a game-show host, dropping full size Kit Kats into our bags.

"Thank you," I say, and am about to turn around and head back home and get Benny cleaned up and get Charlie watered and sort all this good candy, first by type, then by taste, and fall asleep to the smell of chocolate, when a flash of rainbows catches my eye. The recognition is so powerful that I push the front door wide open, stick my head inside, and blurt out, "Sun Joo? Is that you in there? Hey, Sunny!"

As the head turns, it's Sydney's face I see. She glances at me as I peer through her front door like some drooling stalker. She returns her gaze to a mountain of candy surrounded by a circle of girls. She saw me all right, but she acts like she didn't.

"Me Key?"

I hear Sunny's voice. Then I see a small hand waving from the circle. It's Sunny, all right, in Sydney's waitress costume. I don't know why I feel so shocked 'cause I knew they'd be trick-or-treating together. I knew they swapped at school. Sitting next to her are Tammy and Nawsia, sucking on lollipops, whispering into Sunny's ears and giggling. I don't know what they're giggling about, but it makes me mad, makes me want to barge and charge, stomp on their mountain of candy, take my friend away from their hot-as-hell breath contaminating her brain, and cry out, "What kind of stupid name is Nawsia?"

Sydney sees Sunny seeing me, and something triggers. Sydney rushes to the front door. The *hanbok* billows out like a flower blooming in sunshine. It's stunning, as lovely as can be, the kind of pretty that gives you hope, and I think maybe, just maybe, Sydney's coming to the front door to invite me in. But what do I do with Benny and Charlie? I'll have them wait under the flying green-faced witch in the front yard while I catch up with my school friends. It'll only take a minute. As I make plans, tidy my hair, lean into the house, and shift my weight to ready myself for a step inside, Sydney grabs the door and shuts it. *Slam.*

My sticky hope is so stubborn that I think maybe, just maybe, she slipped and ran into the door by accident, and on the count of three, the knob's going to turn and her face is going to show through the crack and she's going to say, "Sorry. Come on in. I didn't mean to do that." One Mississippi. The feathers of the Halloween wreath shiver. Two Mississippi. The ring in the lion's mouth clinkety-clanks. Three Mississippi. His golden eyes blankly stare through me like I'm nothing.

"Who's that?" Benny asks.

"Nobody," I say, taking his hand. The sugar and grime make our palms stick together. We walk down the porch steps.

"She's pretty," he says.

"Shut up," I say, and squeeze his hand hard.

"Owww. I'm telling Ma on you."

"Be my guest, you little snitch. While you're at it, tell her I am sick and tired of doing her job minding you. I ain't your mother. And you're nothing but a thorn in my side, the cross I bear day in and day out. Look at you, Benny. Who do you think you are, all dressed up like a pageant queen? What kind of ridiculous nonsense are you? No wonder Ma don't want to look after you and Daddy don't want to come back," I say, words spilling off my tongue willy-nilly. I press my lips to shut myself up 'cause I'm feeling the rise of my mountain of regrets.

"You're doing ugly," he says.

"You *are* ugly," I say.

"You," he says.

"Your mama," I say.

"Your papa," he says.

"Your sister," I say.

"Your brother," he says.

"Watch it. No one talks about my brother like that," I say.

"You do," he says.

"I know, Benny, and I'm sorry. I feel lousy as a louse."

"You going to beg your pardon?"

"I beg your pardon."

"Okay, but just this once. You hear? Three strikes and you're out."

"I hear."

"She ain't that pretty. She ain't as pretty as you."

"Sounds like you had way too much candy, with all your sweet-talking. Anyway, being pretty ain't all that."

"Yeah. It ain't all that."

"What d'you know about being pretty?"

"A heap more than you," he says, letting go of my hand. He straightens the tiara and shakes his hips, swishing the frills on my pageant dress. He struts a few steps ahead of me, swinging his sack of candy. He throws it over his shoulder, carrying it like Santa.

Charlie and I catch up to him. We get to the inter-section and wait for the cars to zoom by before crossing

Route 12. A dump truck clunks past us, and I know Daddy don't drive a dump truck, but I can't help but wonder if that might be him coming home to tell us another ghost story. Hope is stickier than a chewed-up Now and Later.

Coast is clear. We run across the street.

When we get to our side of Route 12 safe and sound, Benny says, "I'm tired."

I give him a piggyback ride. The tiara keeps slipping off, so he puts it on my head. Benny breathes on my neck. I'm working up a sweat. Our bags of candy sing, plastic wrappers crinkling against one another. Charlie's collar jingles, and his nails scrape against the concrete. I can tell Benny's starting to fall asleep 'cause he's feeling heavier with every step I take. We're almost home. Looks like some folks forgot to draw their blinds, and I spy a TV playing a commercial for Bagel Bites, making me hungry, making me think of all the daddies of the world winding down from a long, long day. A train whistle blows from the other side of town. I hear the distant *chug-chug* along the tracks. If you wish hard enough, it kind of sounds like applause, wild, wild applause.

twenty-three

Why you don't come inside for the trick-or-treat? Sydney say you don't want to see me," Sunny says to me during lunch. We sit at our usual table.

"What are you talking about? That is not true, Sunny. That's a lie. I wanted to come in, but she shut the door in my face, honest to angels," I say.

"Oh? But Sydney say you are mad at me. Are you mad?" Sun Joo opens her lunch box. It's packed with rice and cut-up coins of hot dog.

"No," I say, shaking my head.

"But Sydney say you mad at me because I go to the trick-or-treat with her."

"But Sydney say. But Sydney say. But Sydney say," I mock, bobbing my head.

Sunny scrunches her brows, looks down at my puddle of applesauce, and quietly says, "She say you mad because I not go with you."

"Maybe I was a little upset, but I wouldn't call it

mad. I guess I was kind of disappointed you weren't trick-or-treating with me, but Sydney asked you first. I tried to ask you, but she beat me to it, so I guess that's my bad. First come, first serve, right? Fair is fair. No big deal. I don't really give a flying fart," I say, smothering a soggy fry with ketchup.

"Mickey, I go with you to the trick-or-treat, but you say go with Sydney like that, so I go with Sydney, but I have more fun with you, but you pushing me to go over there because Sydney is like queen and so popular and you want to be popular," she says.

"Excuse you, but I did no such thing. I did not push you to do nothing you didn't already want to do. Maybe you need to grow a spine."

"Grow spine? What you talking?"

"Get a backbone. Don't be such a pushover. Don't be a puppet. Don't say yes, yes, yes to everything," I say, feeling myself inflate all high and mighty.

"I not do that."

"You cling, too. You follow me around like some stray," I say, and for, like, a split second, the taste of saying those words is so sweet, the kind of sweet that blows your brains up, but then in a flash, it all turns sour.

"Sydney say that you using me."

"Using you? Like how? Ain't that a joke."

"You using me to get her."

"Excuse you, honey, but I got no use for you."

Sunny closes her lunch box, packs up her stuff, and says, "Okay. I go."

"Bye," I say, wishing I'd just shut my trap.

I bite into my cheeseburger and watch Sunny walk toward the exit sign. I choke up. I wish I could rewind. I want to follow her, chase her down and say, "I'm an idiot. I'm sorry. I don't know what's wrong with me. This ain't me. Can we be friends again?"

Go. Go. Go. I stand up and start walking, when the Sydney sandwich swoops in and follows Sunny out of the cafeteria.

twenty-four

I got mail. It's not a postcard. It's an honest-to-goodness envelope with something in it. Took Ok long enough to write back. I rip it open. Inside is some kind of church program, I'm guessing, but I can't tell for sure 'cause it's all in Korean except for the small print on the bottom that says "First Korean Full Gospel Church of Greater Washington." That's a mouthful. Ok doodled and scribbled all over it. "Guess where I am?" he wrote. There's a drawing of the preacher at the podium holding up a cross, and the bubble blowing out of his mouth is full of "blah, blah, blah, blah." Under the preacher is a self-doodle of Ok's profile with eyes shut, head hanging low, porcupine hair, and drips of drool turning into a swarm of ZZZZZZZs. Ok finished the letter with: "PS Wear whatever you want. Like you always do. BU."

BU? Oh, I get it. BU as in "be you." That's so corny I like it.

I flip through junk mail, find a Valpak envelope, and

tear it open. I pick the coupon for 10 percent off at Shine Car Wash and start writing on its backside:

Hi!

Today turned decent 'cause I got mail from you. Finally. It cheered me up, and Ma left us a Crock-Pot of beans and rice in bbq sauce. Nothing uplifts the soul like the smell of bbq sauce. Ma's out looking for a job. Remind me never ever to mention getting on welfare to her ever again. She nearly smacked me. "That's not us," she said.

Hey, Ok, I said some not-so-nice things to my new friend, and I think we're like broken up. I don't know what to do. I can't keep my mouth shut. I keep saying the worst things. I stink. I stink worse than cat pee mixed up with throw up.

Speaking of which, do you think you can stay awake long enough in church to pray for Sabrina? I think she's got a case of the cat blues. She's hardly eating anything. Anyway, sorry my letter is so depressing. Here's some good news. I got a birthday around the corner. Hint. Hint. Turning into a teen on 11/20. Mark your calendar. Send something special. I know it's bad manners and all to toot my own birthday, but how you supposed to know if I don't tell you? That's just me being me.

twenty-five

Ms. T's about to start class. Bell rings. Sunny's not here. She never misses class, so I don't know what's up. I saw her in the hall this morning, following Sydney around like life's a game of Simon Says except it's Sydney Says. I wonder if Sunny is skipping. She got herself tangled up with the wrong crowd, and I have to admit that it's kind of my fault. I never should've told her to wear that *hanbok* for Halloween. I never should've pushed her to be friends with Sydney. I made me a monster, didn't I?

Right when Ms. T starts writing on the board, we hear shuffling, giggling, then a loud cackle at the door. In slides Sunny, pushed by Sydney, Tammy, and Nawsia. Sunny belts out a nervous cackle through lips so glossy frosty orange I can't help but think of marmalade sprinkled with mold. All their lips are the same glossy frosty orange. I'll bet they were in the bathroom trying on lipstick.

The others scurry off to their classes, leaving Sunny to quiet down her nervous cackle and take her walk of shame to come sit next to me. But it's not the walk of I'm-so-shy-don't-look-at-me like she did on the first day of school. It's more like the walk of I-now-got-me-some-popular-friends-look-at-me. She's got on a red and black pleated plaid miniskirt with knee-high socks and a red beret on her head. That's bold. Schoolgirl chic.

"I'd like to see you after class, Sun Joo," Ms. T says.

"Ooooooh," the class responds.

"As I was saying, metamorphosis is the biological process . . ."

Sunny sits down, her face looking like she don't give a cat's whisker. Her cheeks don't even flush pink from being embarrassed. It's like she's wearing a mask. She smells different too. It's perfume. As a peace offering, I tear a corner off my paper, write "Love's Baby Soft?" fold the note, and pass it to her.

She reads it, scrunching her brows and squinting her eyes like someone's shining a flashlight into her face. She shrugs.

"Your perfume," I whisper. She tilts her head. "Are you wearing Love's Baby Soft?" What started as a whisper turns into my regular inside voice by the time "Love's Baby Soft" comes out of my mouth. My regular inside voice is kind of loud.

Kids laugh. Ms. T stops talking, clears her throat, and eyes me.

"Sorry," I say.

As Ms. T continues talking about a dragonfly going from a nymph to an adult, Sunny slips her hand into the pocket of her skirt, pulls out a mirror, holds it under our table at just the right angle so she can check her face—more like her mask.

Like some demon's taking over my eyeballs, they rock and roll in their sockets. I don't know why it bugs me so much to see Sunny checking herself out in a mirror. I do it all the time. But that's who I am, and this sure ain't who she is. It's like I'm witnessing this shy, innocent, humble, sweet little caterpillar metamorph into a tangled-up messy cocoon, then metamorph into a cocky butterfly so full of herself that she flutters and flies too close to the birds, thinking she's a bird herself, only to get eaten up by them.

I pass her a note: "How come ur late?"

She reads it and shakes her head.

I pass her a second note: "R U OK?"

She reads it and frowns.

I pass her a third note: "This ain't U."

She reads it, writes on it, and sends it back to me. She crossed out the "ain't" and changed it to "isn't."

I pass her a fourth note: "Ain't. Ain't. Ain't."

She reads it and shakes her head.

I pass her a fifth note: "U changed."

She turns her nose up, stares at Ms. T, and writes back. It says, "We suppose to change."

I add a "d" to "suppose" and send it back.

She crushes the note.

I pass her a sixth note: "Be you."

She writes back, "I am."

I write, "NO. YOU. AIN'T."

She writes, "How you know?"

I write, "'Cause I know."

She writes, "You don't know."

I write, "YOU got no clue."

Sunny takes gum out of her mouth, sticks it in my note, folds it, and slides it to me. The nerve of this girl. Pressing her frosty glossy orange lips together, she stares straight ahead. I slide her nasty gum right back at her. She slides it back, twirling her pen like a baton over her fingers. I used to think that trick was so neat, but now I want her finger to slice off, boomerang across the room, and poke her eye out. I'm about to slide her nasty gum back at her, but she raises her hand. Is she snitching on me? Ms. T calls on her.

Sunny says, "It is the hormone. The hormone make everything to change."

"Exactly. Very good," Ms. T says.

Dead silence. Not one mean word. Not one chuckle from the class. Everyone's in shock. If she was the old Sun Joo, I'd have been so proud of my sweet little friend, but since she's the new and improved Sunny, I want to wipe that smug off her face. Who does she think she is?

Ms. T goes on and on about hormones, but I can't even think straight 'cause I feel lousy as a louse. From the corner of my eye, I watch Sunny taking notes, nodding, raising her hand, asking questions, answering questions, and I'm feeling the way I felt when one sunny summer day, Daddy and Ma and Benny all decided to have an afternoon at the pool without me. I feel left behind. I feel left out.

The bell rings. While packing up, I say, "Listen, Sunny, I'm happy for you. I'm all about live and let live. But I feel the need to tell you that . . ."

She walks away. I am in midsentence, and she walks away. I'm about to go all Ma on her and yell, "Don't you walk away from me, young lady . . . ," but she goes over to the board and talks to Ms. T. I throw my stuff into my backpack and huff-and-puff my way out of class. I was going to humble myself and apologize, but I don't know no more. We are done. We are so done. It's my turn to walk away from this, but then I stop right outside the door, trying to eavesdrop.

I lean in but can't catch anything. Ms. T mumble-jumbles something to Sunny, who doesn't seem to be saying much. I peekaboo through the door crack. I see her backpack and lots of nodding about I don't know what. Then Ms. T hands her some papers and a book.

"Boo."

I jump. I gasp. It's Larry.

"Don't do that," I say.

"Sorry. I didn't mean to scare you."

"You said boo, didn't you? Who says boo without aiming to scare?"

"Right."

"You bet I'm right," I say, getting worked up to give him a piece of my mind, when Sunny comes strolling toward the door. Keeping my eyes on Larry, I smile and giggle so fake I feel sick inside. "You are so funny," I say, and give Larry a shove on his shoulder.

Sunny stops, looks at us, and says, "Me Key?"

I ignore her for three whole seconds, then side-eye her and say, "Oh, you talking to me?"

She nods. Her red beret doesn't budge, staying put on her head like a crown.

"It's Mickey. Not Me Key. Say my name right, why don't you. I'm nobody's key."

"I know," she says.

"No, you don't. YOU got no clue. YOU just got here.

This here's my country 'tis of thee sweet land of liberty. I was here first. You hearing me? Come on, Larry. Let's go," I say, and pull him into the hall.

"I just got used, didn't I? You can let go of my arm now," he says.

I let go.

"Wow. That was really low. What you said to Sun Joo over there. That was pretty bad. Honestly, Mickey, I think you're, like, the coolest girl, but that was not cool," he says.

"You know what's not cool? You breathing down my neck and stalking me since school started. That's what I call pretty bad. Leave me alone, why don't you?" I say.

"Are you all right?" he asks.

"Never been better," I say.

"What's wrong?" he asks.

"Everything," I say, my voice cracking.

"Wow. I'm sorry."

"*Aigo. Aigo.*"

"I what?"

"I go. I have to go," I say, and head into the packed hall.

I pass a locker decorated with balloons and streamers and a sign that says, "Happy Birthday, Dana!" I crack a smile. I love the sight of party supplies. I even love those dumb dunce-party hats that're shaped like cones and the rubber bands break off and slap your face. My favorite store in the whole wide universe is Party Plaza. That's where Daddy would take me to get all my birthday party decorations. He hardly ever made it home on my actual birthdays, but when he was home one or two or three weeks after, it'd be an all-you-can-party-hardy trip to Party Plaza. I didn't even care much about the party part. I was happiest hanging with Daddy up and down those aisles lined with all that shiny shimmering plastic paper goodness. You know how they say laughter's the best medicine? Only second to confetti.

I don't know who this Dana girl is, but what a lucky duck.

I push through a crowd of kids. It's all hustle and bustle, everyone shuffling along to get nowhere. It stinks of cologne, perfume, bad breath, and BO mixed with the general foul odor of school air. My eyes water. My nose runs. What is wrong with me?

twenty-six

Something's wrong. We can't find Sabrina nowhere, not under the couch, not under the beds, not in the closets, not on the windowsills, not in the laundry hamper under the bathroom sink.

"Maybe she gone outside to die," Benny says.

"Shut your piehole, Benny! She hates it outside, and it ain't her time yet, so just shut your piehole," I yell at him.

"There's my girl," Ma says.

She says it so soft and so sweet I have to look at her to make sure it's Ma doing the talking and not some strange Mary Poppins lady who floated out of the sky and into our apartment to soothe and comfort us and help find our cat.

Ma pulls Sabrina out from behind the TV real slow and gentle, while the Teenage Mutant Ninja Turtles do somersaults and backflips on the screen.

"How's our darling," Ma says, cradling the cat in her

arms like a baby. She sounds so soothing and full of love my heart turns to mush. It's like I'm hearing some long-lost voice I used to know from when I was a baby.

Ma sits on the edge of the couch, holding Sabrina and whispering into her ear. My heart beats so loud I can't make out what she's saying. It almost sounds like she's praying in tongues. Benny pets Sabrina, barely touching her, like he knows how dirty his hand is and he's trying not to get her cream fur all grimed up. I kneel and stroke her neck. We all got our hands on her like the way preachers do when they try to heal the sick.

"Is she dying?" Benny asks.

"I think so," Ma whispers.

"No, Ma. No," I say, tears falling out of my eyes. I can't breathe right.

"It's okay," Benny says, and pats my shoulder with his nasty hand.

"You go on, sweet baby. We'll be all right," Ma tells Sabrina.

"No," I say.

"Bye, Sabrina. I'm going to miss you. Have fun in pussy heaven," Benny says.

My eyes are blurry with tears, but when Benny says that, I look up at Ma and Ma looks down at me, and we smile so big that we crack up laughing.

"Hope they got a lot of cockroaches up there. That'll keep you plenty busy," Benny says.

"That's gross, Benny," I say, elbowing him like I'm annoyed, but I'm not. I'm so grateful he lightened my heavy sadness.

I lay my cheek on Sabrina's warm body. Her breathing's slow.

"Bye, girl," I say.

And then, just like that, our cat stops breathing. Sabrina's gone. She goes lifeless limp in Ma's arms. And I'm sad, but also surprised how light I feel, how it don't hurt like a stubbed toe or a scraped knee or a broken bone. It's almost sweet. I picture her spirit floating above, seeing us huddled and loving on her, and I get a strong sense of what it looks like to rest in peace.

twenty-seven

A plate of fake Oreo cookies from the Dollar Store and two glasses of milk are sitting on the table when me and Benny get home from school. This is downright weird, but we drop everything, rush over, and munch-gulp-crunch like Cookie Monster.

Ma never does stuff like this. This here's the stuff she makes fun of other mothers for doing. She's the kind to order us to get our own cookies and milk. *Who do you think I am? Your slave?*

Ma comes out of her bedroom, walks over to us, and sets down a CD by my stack of cookies. It's my dance CD, the one I left playing at Golden Gardens.

"I got that job," Ma says.

"I knew it, Ma! I knew you could do it. Didn't I tell you?"

"I owe you, Mickey. That manager Jerry? I had an interview with him. He remembered me from that night we were dancing in the lobby. We hit it off. Some of the seniors remembered me too. They called me Gidget's mom. I got hired on the spot. I start tomorrow. You're looking at the new events coordinator for Golden Gardens Assisted Living."

I scream, jumping up and down.

"Are we going to be rich?" Benny asks.

"Ma, that's the best news!" I say.

"I don't know about rich, but we should be better off. Some bills are going to get caught up. Maybe new shoes."

"I want a new bike," says Benny.

"Slow down. First paycheck don't come for three weeks. Things are still going to be tight around here, so I'm aiming to pawn and sell some stuff. We got too much junk," Ma says, looking around the apartment.

I put a cookie in my mouth, get up, and pop my CD into the player.

Abba spills into the room, singing about the dancing queen. Benny stands on the chair, cookie in each hand, and shakes his butt, having the time of his life. Charlie wags his tail and barks. Ma kicks up her legs like she's dancing the Charleston in slow motion. I twirl, spinning around the room to the beat of the tambourine, feeling young and sweet and dizzy with relief.

twenty-eight

Where do I sit? It's gone," Benny says on the morning of my thirteenth birthday.

"You don't got time to sit. We need to get to school," I say.

Ma got rid of Daddy's La-Z-Boy recliner. There's a square of fade on the carpet, which shows like one of those "I was here" signs. Ma sold it to Mr. Doug downstairs 'cause we need the money. Ma's been on a rampage pawning our stuff. I noticed all her jewelry's gone, including her wedding rings. I offered up all my pageant dresses, tiaras, shoes, trophies—all of it—to turn to dough. She's cleaning house and cashing in.

I been telling myself not to expect nothing for my thirteenth. She ain't cashing in to buy me nothing. She ain't throwing me a fancy party. She's getting late bills paid, trying to keep us from getting evicted until her first paycheck.

"Evicted" means to get kicked out of your home 'cause

you can't pay up. All your stuff gets thrown outside like trash into one big heap for all the world to see and pity.

I seen this happen at Parkside Gardens. People's stuff thrown outside like garbage. Sofas, chairs, tables, lamps, mattresses, microwaves with food still cooking inside, trash bags upon trash bags. They don't even give them time to pack proper. The saddest is seeing toys. Stuffed elephants and bears tossed to the curb. Board games tossed out, their boxes spilled open. All those itty-bitty game pieces separated and scattered. And the people getting evicted just stand around too shocked and too sad and too mad and too lost to do nothing but hang their heads while their home gets flipped inside out. Never mind their belongings. What about them? They got nowhere to go.

"What's in your bag?" Benny asks as we walk to his bus stop.

"Stuff for my birthday," I say.

"Happy Birthday, dear Mickey, happy birthday to you," sings Benny.

Before tears bust out of my eyes, I say, "Don't you know the words to the whole song? Never you mind, 'cause you sing like Charlie on helium."

"I got you something," Benny says. He pulls a wad of toilet paper out of his pocket and hands it to me.

"What? Birthday boogers?"

"Open it."

Inside the wad is what I gather used to be a stick of Kit Kat. The chocolate's melted, and the cookie part is crumbs.

"It's your favorite. It's the last of my Halloween candy. I saved it for you," he says, proud like he just saved a life.

"Oh, Benny. This here's the sweetest and the most disgusting thing ever. Kind of like you," I say, wrapping the crushed candy.

"Aren't you eating it?"

"Saving it for later."

"Happy birthday."

"Silly boy. Come here."

He leans into me. His hair smells like home: dogs and cats and cigarettes and pancakes mixed up with that odor you get playing outside in November air. My eyes water. Thanksgiving's around the corner. Daddy used to insist on birthday cake and candles for Thanksgiving dessert 'cause of me. He was late for everything most of the time, a better-late-than-never kind of daddy, so when he did show up after the fact, he went all out to make up for it 'cause he'd have a bad case of the guilts.

"Don't miss your bus. Get going," I say, and send Benny along.

As I walk to my stop, I check my grocery bag of birthday stuff, hoping it's enough. Without a trip to

Party Plaza, I didn't have much to work with. I have to make do with what I got. And what I got ain't a lot. Nothing bought. But better than snot. Making birthday happiness from rot.

Big and fancy was never my aim for my birthdays. My heart of hearts was set on Ma and Daddy walking into my classroom, disturbing a boring lesson with a tray of cupcakes for everyone. And the class would cheer wild. The time I saw this happen was in Ms. Clarke's second-grade class with John Jerome Malcolm's parents barging in during a spelling test. They brought a Carvel ice-cream cake, and John Jerome's dad in his booming voice told Ms. Clarke and all of us, "Stop! Pencils down! This can't wait! Ice cream is melting!" Whole class lost it. John Jerome looked like he was trying to look embarrassed, but you can't hide true joy. Happiness beamed through his brown eyes. We chucked our spelling tests. We scream-sang "Happy Birthday." We ate ice-cream cake. It was the joy to top all joys. Even the shy, quiet kids had smiles on their faces.

That was my birthday wish. To do like John Jerome. I tried to get Ma and Daddy on board, but with Daddy on the road and Ma sleeping days, the best I could pull off was a box of animal crackers, most of which was missing body parts.

In fifth grade, I was so determined to make my

birthday dreams come true even a little bit, I made cherry Jell-O the night before to share with everyone in my class. I even rounded up some used candles to blow out making my birthday wishes. I imagined everyone singing "happy birthday to Mickey, happy birthday to you," as I wiggled and jiggled the tub of Jell-O. We'd slurp it. We'd squish it between our teeth. We'd gargle it. We'd have ourselves a fun mess of a time. But when I got to school, the Jell-O was melting fast, a layer of red liquid forming on the surface. By afternoon, my birthday Jell-O was more like birthday blood. I ended up pouring it down the toilet in the girls' bathroom along with my birthday fantasies.

This time, older and wiser, I'm better prepared.

As I run into the school building, I'm still holding out an electron of hope that maybe, just maybe, someone might could have beat me to it. My locker might be decorated. You never know. There's always a chance.

I turn down my hall and run to locker 1582. Nothing. Same old gray metal door. Fine by me, 'cause I came prepared to take care of my birthday myself.

I dig into my grocery bag of birthday stuff. I cover my locker door with pieces of old wrapping paper. I got to hurry my butt before kids spill into the halls. My door ends up looking like an old patched-up quilt of balloons, flowers, birthday cakes, and Santa heads. I like it.

I tape up the puffy flowers I made with twisty ties and tissues. I tape up the letters of my birthday sign above my locker. H-A-P-P-Y-B-I-R-T-H-D-A-Y-M-I-C-K-E-Y-! I cut them out from old greeting cards. I even cut up my favorite Strawberry Shortcake birthday card Daddy gave me for my sixth. It's now a big capital *M*. I love how mismatched everything looks. It's a hodgepodge of a mess, a real work of art, if you ask me.

Now for the finishing touch, the crowning glory. I tape pieces of my Halloween candy all over my locker door so anyone can help themselves to a sweet treat. I can't believe I didn't pig out on all this candy myself. I tape the last piece, a bag of M&M's, to the bottom left corner and step back to admire my work. Best decorated locker ever, if I do say so myself.

"You did it, Mickey. Happy thirteenth. Make it good," I say, and watch the clock.

As I wait for the bell to scream, it's dawning on me that my days of little-girl innocence are long gone. A rose ain't just a rose no more. I was never one to get suckered into being naive, so I guess it's like my number finally caught up to me, but boy am I going to miss being free of cares. Closest I'll come to carefree is a box of panty shields.

It's like a part of me has to die so another part can live.

The bell screams.

The faraway echo of voices and footsteps starts to fill the hall. My heart beats fast. I'm excited. I'm kind of scared, too. It feels like I'm waiting for everyone to arrive at my party. It also feels like I'm waiting for a stampede to run me over. I stand next to my locker, practicing one of those lookie-here poses, jazz hands and all.

Here they come.

A sixth-grade boy stops, looks, and asks, "Can I have one?"

"Sure! But just one. And you have to wish me a happy birthday."

He pulls off a Baby Ruth and says, "Happy birthday, Mickey."

"Thanks," I say.

"Hey, happy birthday," Justin says, and grabs a Snickers.

"Thanks."

"No, thank you."

"Is it free?" someone asks.

"It's free. You just have to wish me a happy birthday."

"Happy birthday!"

"This is so cool."

"I love this idea."

"Happy birthday, Mickey!"

I see Frankie "Doo-Doo" Dooley coming this way. He's going to say something mean. I know it. He stops, stares, and asks, "If I wish you happy birthday twice, can I get two?"

"Sure," I say.

"Happy birthday. Happy birthday," he says, taking only one piece.

"Thanks, Frankie," I say.

Birthday wishes come pouring in as candy gets pulled off my locker. I feel like a talking vending machine. I feel really good. I feel joyous. It's like a star's burning inside me, and I'm all shine.

I'm down to the last seven pieces when Sydney, Tammy, Nawsia, and Sunny come marching down the hall like they have to investigate what all the commotion is about. They stop in front of my locker. They're all wearing matching black velvet chokers around their necks, which remind me of Charlie's collar. Sydney may as well hold a leash. Up and down and up go Sydney's eyes like a seesaw. She sees my locker, and she aims to saw me to pieces.

"What's all this?" she asks.

"It's my birthday," I say, jazzing my hands.

"Oh. Wow. Who did this?"

"Me."

"You decorated your own locker for your birthday," she says, bobbing her head like a chicken.

"So?"

"It's sad."

"It's called taking care of myself," I say.

"You do realize it's your friends who are supposed to be taking care of this for you? You're not supposed to decorate your own locker. That's really pathetic. Don't you have any friends?" she says, hissing the s.

"Oh look! She has M&M's," Nawsia says, reaching down to pull them off.

"Don't," Sydney says, kicking Nawsia's hand away.

"Oww," Nawsia says, standing up.

"It's old Halloween candy, dummy. It's expired. It'll make your skin break out, and you of all people don't need that," says Sydney.

"It's like she's a big Pez dispenser," says Tammy.

"Good one, but she's more like the cannibal witch in *Hansel and Gretel*. This is, like, a total trap," Sydney says.

"Some kids behind you want candy, so can you move along?" I say.

"It's like you're luring them with candy just so you can eat them up because obviously you eat just about everything," she says, smiling and looking at her girls.

"Go on a diet," says Nawsia.

"You would be pretty if you weren't so fat," says Tammy.

"It's not healthy," says Sydney.

My jazz hands go all clenched fists. Sydney's getting to me, and I don't want her to. My head heats up.

"Mickey! Mickey! I like this one. Can I have?" Sunny says, pushing through the Sydney sandwich. She reaches for a Hershey's Kiss. "Happy birthday, Mickey."

"Thanks, Sunny. There's another Hershey's Kiss over here, too. You can have it," I say, getting choked up. I missed her so much I want to hug her.

"Everybody, let's sing to Mickey! Let's sing the 'Happy Birthday' song! Happy birthday to you," Sunny starts to sing.

Sydney steps in, puts her hand over Sunny's mouth, and shushes her, saying, "Joo Joo, no. Please. Mickey doesn't need us to sing. She takes care of herself. She's a big girl."

A small crowd has gathered, clogging up the hall and waiting for us to fight. I do not want to fight. I just want to give out free candy. I take a deep breath. These kids want a showdown.

"Oh my God. I feel so sorry for you," Sydney says.

"Likewise. I feel sorry for you, too, Sydney," I say as sweet as I can, 'cause sometimes sweet burns.

"Oh, how original of you. I guess you want to copy

me in everything. Admit it. You want to be just like me."

"Ooooooh," the kids say.

"I guess that would be true if I wanted to be, oh, I don't know, mean and petty and insecure and snotty with a bloated head. News flash. I do not want to be anything like you, Sydney. I know what you're all about. You put me down so you can feel better about yourself. I don't feel the need to do that to anyone, not even you. I got names for you, oh, do I have names for you, but I choose to restrain myself from using them 'cause that would be downright low and mean. Instead, I do stuff like decorate my own locker and give out free candy 'cause it makes me feel good about myself. What's it to you that I mind who I am? I know me, and I sure as heaven don't need everyone else squattin' down low for me to stand tall and mighty. So bless your crooked little gizzard, sweetheart. Now, excuse you," I say.

"Ooooooh," the kids say.

Clapping starts up in the back. It's Larry. Sunny claps too. Sydney throws her an evil eye, but others start applauding too. I'm getting applauded on my birthday for telling Sydney off.

"Settle. Settle. Break it up. Get to your classes," Mr. Graves booms, just in time to kill my joy. Everyone scatters.

The bell rings.

As I open my locker for my backpack, someone taps my shoulder. It's probably Larry here to collect on a thank-you for starting up the applause, so I take my time turning around. It's not him. It's Sunny.

"Happy Birthday, Mickey. Did I say right?" she says.

"Close enough, Sun Joo. Is that right?"

She nods.

"Joo Joo?"

"I know. But Sydney say it sound cute. I'm sorry, Mickey."

"I'm sorry too," I say, and give her a wink like my daddy used to do, but what I really want to do is give her a hug and tell her how much I miss her and why aren't we friends anymore and I'm sorry for bugging her with those stupid notes and I'm happy for her, I really am, and I'm all about living your best no matter what trials and tribulations life throws your way, whether it's coming to a new country or trying to fit in or learning a new language or being you or a runaway daddy or losing a friend or a sick cat or worrying about getting kicked out of your home, or this or that or did I mention I miss you . . .

Instead I say, "Hey, want these? I know it's your favorite."

I pull all the Hershey's Kisses off my locker and hand them to her.

Sun Joo takes them and says, "You giving me the *ddong*."

"*Ddong* mention it," I say.

"Ha-ha," she says, and walks away.

I close my locker and admire my scrappy door, proud of how I helped myself. The *M* in my name falls off the wall, leaving the sign HAPPY BIRTHDAY ICKEY. I laugh. I pick up the *M* cut out from that Strawberry Shortcake birthday card from Daddy way back, when I loved all things Strawberry Shortcake. She was sweet and cute, sugar and spice, and all things nice, kind of like dessert. On the backside is some of his writing all cut up. "To my ba rthday lov ways Da." Ain't that a poem? Da. Da. I'm not a baby no more. I tape the letter back up and walk to class, feeling lucky thirteen and as sweet as snakes and snails and puppy-dog tails.

twenty-nine

"Why are we here?" I ask as Ma parks at the Prince George's County Animal Shelter.

"You just wait right here," she says, grabbing her purse. She gets out of the car, shuts the door, and stands under a tree for a smoke.

Benny and I are in the back seat with Charlie lying across our laps. She's done this to us before, but we never made it this far 'cause we ran out of gas. My stomach goes all queasy with dread. I hug Charlie and tell him that we ain't going to let nothing happen to him. Over my dead body.

Out the window, I see Ma blowing smoke. She's in her Golden Gardens work clothes 'cause she's working later today. She's been clipping coupons, skipping meals, scrimping and saving to tide us over until her first paycheck, but it's still not enough. It's never enough. Look at her blowing smoke like a chimney. She can't quit the cigs. Those aren't cheap. And if she gets lung cancer, we're going to end up homeless paying hospital bills. She's always yelling at us not to end up in the ER 'cause it's going to cost an arm and two legs, but look at her puffing all her money away. I have a mind to open the window and yell some sense at her, but something about the way she stands out there all alone under the tree with its leaves hanging on for dear life makes me think twice, makes me wish her cigarette could last forever.

But it don't, and she smokes it down to the butt and throws it away. As she walks over to us, I lock the car. She shakes her head, pulls out her keys, unlocks the doors, and holds ours open to see us out.

"No, Ma. I can't let you do this," I say, as Charlie pulls me out of the back seat.

"Let me? Since when do you let me do anything?" she says, and shuts the door.

"Ma, please. Pretty please. I beg you," I say, following her across the parking lot.

"What'd I tell you about begging?"

"Not to."

"Then why am I hearing all this please, please, pretty please nonsense? It don't become you, Mick. It's downright ugly."

Ugly is one of them words that puts a spell on me. It's my kryptonite. It's got some voodoo magic that knocks me down and sinks me into a quiet shame. I shut up.

"Are you selling Charlie to the pound?" Benny asks.

"Pounds don't buy dogs. They take them for free," she says.

"You're giving him away for free?" he asks.

"Benny, who said anything about giving Charlie away?" Ma's voice sounds like one of them kindergarten teachers trying to explain death by saying it's just like a vacation to Candy Land. *Your grandpa's in Candy Land.*

I can't stand it, so I run my mouth ugly.

"Don't lie, Ma. You said it. You did. You've been getting rid of all our stuff. Now you're getting rid of Charlie," I say.

Ma breathes out so deep she might deflate and melt into a sack of skin right in front of our eyes. I brace myself for a smack, 'cause she's done it before. Ain't nothing keeping her from doing it again. She can beat me to a pulp, see if I care. If it means keeping Charlie with us another few minutes, fine by me. Like I told him, over my dead body.

"Please, Ma. We just lost Sabrina. I can't bear to lose no more. Why can't we keep him? Ma. Please. I'll do anything. I'll clean. I'll make dinner every night. I won't sass back. I'll look after Benny. I'll clean out the litter box every day. Every single day, Ma. I swear. Cross my heart," I say.

"Charlie's going to be fine. Please calm yourself down, Mick. And what'd I say about making promises you can't keep?" she says, walking through the front doors.

I squat down, put my arm around Charlie's neck, unhook his leash, and tell him to make a run for it. "Go, boy, go. I'd rather you be free than end up in the pound. It's death row for old dogs. So get out of here!" I say, and stand up. He don't move. I give him a nudge with my knee, but instead of running for the hills, he follows Ma into the pound. Then Benny follows Charlie, and I'm the only one left outside.

Through the glass doors I see Ma talking to a girl at the front desk. The girl nods and smiles and hands her a clipboard. Benny jumps up and down like he's throwing a tantrum. Charlie stands next to Ma, wagging his tail. He's got no clue what's going on. I have to stop this.

The doors slide open. I march to the smiling girl at the front desk. Her name tag says "Charity." Before I can say, "Listen here, Charity. There's been a mistake," she pops up like a jack-in-the-box and sings out, "Happy birthday!"

"What? Why? How'd you know?"

"Your mom," she says, pointing her out in the waiting area like I don't know who my own mother is.

"You think going around telling strangers to wish me a happy birthday is going to make up for the fact that you're throwing out a member of our family? Some nerve, Ma. Some nerve. It's downright cruel."

Benny jumps up and down, covering his mouth with one hand and pointing at me with the other. Ma's head is down, filling out papers. Charlie stares at me. Something's weird.

"Ma!" I call out.

"What now, Mickey?" she says without looking up from the clipboard.

"I don't understand why you have to go around telling strangers it's my . . ."

Ma stands up and walks over to the front desk. She hands the clipboard to Charity, who looks over the sheets of paper, then says, "Everything looks good! Right this way. The cats are in this room."

"Cats?"

Benny pushes me and says, "Gotcha! Gotcha good!"

"What's going on? We're getting a cat? Ma? What about Charlie? We ain't giving him away? Why's he here? Ma?" I ask, trying to keep up with her.

"Charlie has to get along with our new cat. Don't you remember Kelly hissing and scratching at him for months? Can't let that happen again."

"Ma," I say, my voice cracking.

She looks down at me and smiles, shaking her head like she don't know what to do with me. She says, "I'm expecting you to keep all those promises you made. What was it? Litter box cleaned every day?"

"I'm sorry, Ma."

"No need, Mickey. I thought it was mighty of you protecting Charlie like that. That was strong."

"Thanks, Ma."

As we follow Charity down the hall, the walls spin like I'm on some topsy-turvy ride at a carnival. It's all blurry except for Ma's back, the only thing I'm seeing in focus. She stands straight like a dagger. I don't know how she keeps her posture pageant perfect like that after all those nights hunched in a tollbooth. Tap-tap go Charlie's nails against the linoleum floor. Benny skips. Ma chats with Charity. I suddenly feel like holding Ma's hand. I don't know how long it's been. I was little. I know that. And it was probably 'cause Daddy's hand wasn't around. It was always his hand I'd choose to hold. Ma never got picked by me. I reach over and take her hand. She takes mine and holds tight like it's something we do.

thirty

I have been dying to write Ok with a news flash that's going to make his jaw drop to the soles of his stinky feet, but it hasn't been my turn. We got a ping-pong thing going. I ping. He pongs. I ping back. He pongs back. Can't throw it off and ping, ping, ping. But finally I got mail from Ok today. It's a big bumpy pink Hallmark envelope. I rip it open, and all this confetti and glitter fall out all over the place. I empty the rest of the envelope on my head, and for a few seconds it's snowing Party Plaza.

He got the confetti and glitter part right, but the card looks like something you'd send to a grandma. A bouquet of pink flowers shaped into a heart. It *is* a card for a grandma! On the front, it says "Birthday Blessings for Grandma." Inside there's a Bible verse. "The Lord bless thee and keep thee. The Lord make his face shine upon thee." I laugh 'cause this has got to be Ok's idea of a joke. I flip to the back side, and I can't believe he spent a whopping $3.98 on this Hallmark birthday card for grandmas.

Happy Birthday, Mickey.

Sorry about the card. I know you're not my grandma, but my mom got it, and she saw it was pretty and didn't pay attention to the words. It's the last time I ask her to pick anything out for me. I hope you think it's funny. That part about the Lord making his face shine on you? Isn't that weird? It makes me think of Jesus in a toothpaste commercial, laser beaming his sparkling white teeth at people. I don't think you need it, I mean his laser light to beam on thee because thee know how to shine on thine own. Don't get any ideas that I sent you a big pink card with a heart on it. Like I said, it's my mom's fault. Happy birthday.

Your grandson,

Ok

I want to write back so bad that I don't bother making a card. I rip a sheet out of my spiral notebook and start writing:

Hey Ok,

Remember that time you ran away? And there was that cat with one eye? Remember how that cat saved your butt from being all alone in that sad tent you called home? Remember how that cat kept you warm? Remember how she was just the sweetest little thing? You ever wonder what happened to that cat? Well, wonder no more. 'Cause guess what? News flash! She's here with us! She's ours! We adopted Cyclops! We brought her home from the pound! What?! How? Where? Why? When? you ask.

Long story short, Sabrina died, and it broke our hearts. You probably don't remember Sabrina 'cause she'd go and hide when you came over. She didn't like you too much. Don't take it personal 'cause sometimes she didn't like us too much either. Anyway, after she went to kitty heaven, I would not have dreamed of asking for another cat even though we were always a three-cat, one-dog family and it was my thirteenth birthday, 'cause Ma was getting rid of all our stuff, I mean all our stuff, and I swear she was aiming to get rid of Charlie, but oh boy was I wrong. We got Cyclops! And in the nick of time, I tell you, 'cause the pound was getting ready to put her on death row 'cause she'd been there for a while and no one wants a one-eyed cat. Except yours truly.

I'd take an old one-eyed cat over a fresh cute kitten any old day 'cause here's how I figure it. That cute little kitten's going to have a loving home because people love cute little kittens with two eyes. People will fight over a kitten, but a cat like Cyclops missing an eye don't have a chance. She's a reject. No one's going to fight for her. And you know what's sadder than dying? Dying alone and unwanted. I think that's just the saddest.

I was sad that Sabrina died, but she took her last breath in Ma's arms, and me and Benny were there by her side saying good-bye and loving on her. I know she felt that. Everyone should feel that.

This whole thing's gotten me thinking about life and how life is about losing stuff and getting stuff back. You know what I mean? Think about it. If we didn't lose Sabrina, we wouldn't have Cyclops. And Cyclops would be dead. And if you didn't lose your daddy, you wouldn't have what you got today. And if I didn't lose my daddy, I wouldn't have . . . well, I don't know what I wouldn't have 'cause that blank ain't all filled yet, but knowing that something's going to fill it one of these days makes me feel better. Get what I'm saying? Anyway, here's to being 13 and being me.

Your grandma,
Mickey

PS *There are way too many strays at the pound. Save a cat. Adapt. (I know it's adopt, but adopt don't rhyme with cat unless you want a cot.)*

PPS *Knock, knock. Who's there? Thanks. Thanks who? Thanks to you, I got to go vacuum now.*

thirty-one

This morning's announcement said to meet in Mr. Jankowski's art room during lunch if you wanted to help plan the winter dance. Sydney's voice came through the speaker. "Your president Sydney Stevenson here. Good morning! With our winter dance right around the corner, we need your creative ideas for making this year's dance the best ever, so let's do lunch and have ourselves a storm of brains! But only if you're, like, serious about helping out."

When she said "storm of brains," I saw brains pouring down out of the sky like rain, then collecting and spinning into a tornado swirl over Landover Hills Middle. I wouldn't miss this storm of brains for a Crock-Pot of Ma's mashed potatoes. I missed the dance last year 'cause Benny was burning up with a fever of 104, and guess who had to make sure he didn't die? Yep. Nurse Mickey to the rescue. Come hell or high water,

I'm not missing it this year. Besides, anything beats lunch in the cafeteria.

I walk into Mr. Jankowski's art room with my tray of food. Looks like I'm late since I had to wait in line to get lunch. Everyone else has bag lunches and cans of soda from the vending machine. I guess sloppy joes are too sloppy for this gathering of Sydney's followers. Sunny sits near the front with her own bag lunch and a can of Orange Crush. Sydney sits at the blackboard on Mr. Jankowski's stool with a can of Diet Coke. Seeing me, she says, "For those of you coming late, take a seat in the back."

There's an empty seat in the front near the door, so I take that one instead.

"That seat's reserved. You can't sit there," she says, and sips her Diet Coke.

"Why not?"

"Because you're not handicapped. That's the handicap seat."

I open my pint of chocolate milk and chug it down. When Sydney sees I got no mind to sit in the back, she says, "I guess disabilities come in all shapes and sizes."

Someone spits out her soda.

Someone giggles.

Someone says, "Oh my God. That's, like, mean, Syd. Be nice."

I take a big bite of my sloppy joe to keep myself from saying something offensive, something I might regret. I chew my food. I feel the bun sticking to the roof of my mouth. Sauce runs down my wrist. I got two halves of a maraschino cherry in my fruit cocktail. You're pretty lucky if you get one half, so I'm choosing to count my cherries. I finish off my chocolate milk and burp.

They all look at me.

"Pardon," I say, and lick off my milk mustache.

"As I was saying, we need a theme for the dance," Sydney says.

"Masquerade!"

"But that's so Halloween," Sydney says.

"Let's just stick with the Winter Wonderland theme."

"But that's so boring. They do that every year. I want this year to be special. I want to start some new traditions. I really want to leave a mark. Like I want it to have my signature on it, if you know what I mean," says Sydney.

"This isn't the Sydney Show," says Tammy.

"But it is," Sydney says, and flips her hair.

"Ha-ha."

"Disney?"

"What are we, like in second grade?"

"How about we call it Avalanche and just bury everyone in snow?"

"Yeah, Snowmageddon."

"Snow Monster Ball. That would be so cool."

"No," says Sydney.

"You keep shooting everything down. Do you have any bright ideas?" asks Tammy.

"I do. I'm so glad you asked. Saving the best for last. Okay, so, I've, like, thought about this, like a lot, and it's like a personal dream of mine. Are you ready? I really think that we should do . . . drumroll . . ."

We wait.

Sydney pops off the stool, jumps, pumps one fist in the air like she's cheerleading, and shouts, "Aspen!"

The room is struck silent. This storm of brains has hit the fan.

"Ass what?" someone asks.

"Aspen, dummy, as in ski resorts for the rich and famous? Mountains of Colorado? Don't you know anything?"

"Have you been there?"

"Yeah, like every winter practically. I'm kind of getting bored of it, but I feel like this dance needs that special magical flare. It needs a major upgrade. I want it to be posh and luxurious and have that exclusive membership sort of feel. I envision, like, this welcome-to-Aspen ski-lodge theme with logs for walls and a great big stone fireplace and an ice sculpture of our mascot and a snow machine so that it's, like, snowing on the dance floor, and for our pièce de résistance, a ski lift."

"We could have snow cones, too."

"And a chocolate fountain."

"We should make s'mores in the fireplace."

"And fur! I want fur. Like a big bear rug in front of the fireplace and fur trim on dresses. This is going to be so awesome. Welcome to Aspen!" Sydney says.

I choke on my cherries. I clear my throat and blurt out, "How much is this going to cost? Who's going to pay for it?"

All heads turn to look at me except Sydney's. She smiles and says to her followers, "Oh, now that she's done stuffing her face with sloppy joes, the girl speaks. This goes for everyone—please keep all your comments constructive and positive. Otherwise, as president, I have the right to dismiss anyone out of my meeting."

"Hey, Syd, she kind of has a point. Aspen sounds amazing, but it sounds really expensive," someone says.

The room's so quiet you could hear the clock tick.

"I really don't need any of this negativity. We'll find the money. The school can do, like, those fund-raisers. And we're charging for tickets. We'll charge more than usual. Where there's a will, there's a way. Money is no object. We can make this happen, guys. Dream with me. Besides, I'm not hearing any other brilliant ideas."

"I got an idea," I say, and raise my hand.

"No, we are not doing a hoedown," says Sydney, holding her palm out to stop me.

Some laugh.

"Syd, be nice," says Tammy, giggling.

"I'm trying," says Sydney, sipping her Diet Coke.

"What is your idea, Mickey?" asks Sunny.

"Thanks, Sunny. Well, I was at the pound the other day, and I'm happy to announce we adopted a cat. Name is Cyclops McDonald. She's only got one eye, but she's the cutest thing. I don't know if y'all been to the pound lately, but that place is packed with cats and dogs. You know what happens to these guys if they can't find a home? They get put down. I don't know about y'all, but that really bugs me. Why don't we help save some lives? I propose we call our school dance the Winter Rescue Dance. We can donate some of the money from ticket sales to the shelter. We can raise awareness. Maybe we can even hook the dogs and cats up with loving families! We can ask the pound to bring cats and dogs to the dance. And heck, we can invite our families, too, so they can all come and dance and meet the cats and dogs and maybe even take one home. Sydney, you know that mark you're aiming to make? Well, hot dang, believe you me, this here Winter Rescue Dance is going to put you on the map," I say, and toss my milk carton into the trash can. Score. As I gather my things and start heading to the door, I add, "Heck, I wouldn't be surprised if you get on the local news for being some kind of hero."

As I make my grand exit, I hear them talking.

"That would be, like, so cool."

"I want a dog."

"I want a cat."

I want to eavesdrop at the door, but I don't. I keep going on my merry way, 'cause deep down I don't mind what they say about me and my ideas. I'm not hungry for applause. I feel full. The hall's empty. It's quiet out here. Bell's about to ring any second now. For the first time in a long time, I feel the cloud-nine lightness of not giving a rat's rectum what they think of me. I feel free.

thirty-two

It's Family Day at Golden Gardens Assisted Living. The only reason me and Benny are here is 'cause Ma promised us cupcakes and punch. Since she's now the events coordinator, she has to make sure Family Day runs smooth. If you don't got family dropping by to say hi, that's where me and Benny come in. Ma said to play like we're someone's grandkids 'cause some of these seniors got no one visiting. So we sit, chat, play checkers, play cards, eat cupcakes, and sip punch, which has in it lime sherbet, lemon slices, and maraschino cherries. It's the kind of punch that's so good, it knocks out the cupcake in the first round.

As I pour myself another cup, I spy a glossy black toupee that brings to mind strands of licorice. I recognize this man. As he limps toward the table with a cane, I say, "I know you. You're Superman."

He stops, takes a real good look at me, tapping his cane, and says, "Gidget? Is that you?"

I burst out laughing, nearly spitting out my punch. I wasn't expecting him to remember me. As he picks up a cup with a shaky hand, he says, "What's your name?"

"Mickey," I say.

"I'm Herman, but you can call me Superman," he says.

"Okay."

"This is how I'm going to remember your name." He starts to sing the *Mickey Mouse Clubhouse* theme song.

I join in, and together we sing "M-O-U-S-E."

"What a bunch of brats. Catchy song, but annoying-as-hell kids. Don't be like that, Mickey," he says, reaching into his jacket pocket.

"No, sir," I say, and pour him some punch.

He pours half the punch back into the bowl, pulls out a flask, opens it with his shaky hands, pours a splash of something else into his punch, and says, "Keeps me going."

He walks to a table near the window. I follow with his cupcake. He moves slower than a snail drenched in Elmer's. And he's spilling punch all over the carpet. I'm reaching to take his cup, when a talon swoops in and grabs it. It's not a real talon. It's a hand, but it may as well be the talon of some fancy-pants exotic bird, pet to some fancy-pants Queen Shebalicious, because the bony fingers are tipped with long shiny red nails and decorated in rings with gems so gigantic, candy Ring Pops come to mind.

"Herman, are you baptizing the carpets again?" an old woman asks, and sips Herman's punch. "You naughty man," she says, and takes another sip.

"Who are you here for, darling?" she asks me.

"My ma works here. She's right over there," I say.

"Colleen's your mother? Oh, I like Colleen. Bless her heart. She had us dancing the Electric Slide. She's nicer than that other one we had. What was her name, Herman? Oh, she was a mean one. She'd just sit us in front of a television set and sometimes forget to turn it on. We'd wait and wait and wait, and the next thing we know, she'd gone home for the day. But I like your mother. She keeps us entertained. But she really ought to do something about that dreadful hair of hers. Sweetheart, now tell me something. Have you received Jesus Christ as your personal Lord and Savior?" she says, taking my hand and squeezing it. Her bracelets jingle.

"Yes, ma'am. Praise the Lord," I say.

"Darling, do you see that man over there at the door? That's my son. Look how handsome he is, but I do wish he wouldn't slouch so much. It takes two inches off his height. A man has to stand proud and tall," she says.

I wave my arms, and the man sees us. Once he starts

walking over, I tell the woman to have a nice visit and walk away.

I look for Benny. He's sitting at a table in the back corner. An old lady with an Easter hat talks to him, but he's busy stuffing his face with a cupcake, licking chocolate frosting off his fingers. The room is filling up with all kinds of folks, old and young. I guess that's family for you. Music's playing in the background, but fading fast as voices take over. It's a nice room. The fancy wallpaper and carpet and curtains remind me of a fairy-tale ballroom, but it don't feel anything like happily ever after here. It's kind of boring and sad. And I feel kind of sorry, like how I felt for the cats and dogs at the shelter. It's like they're both stuck somewhere they don't really want to be, waiting around for who knows what.

Ma pours more ginger ale into the punch bowls. She looks real nice in her red blouse and black skirt. And her hair don't look bad. It looks real pretty, and I feel proud of her for making Family Day happen for everyone.

A man standing at the doors makes me do a double take 'cause I swear he could pass for Daddy from across the room, and I wonder if Ma feels how Daddy's not here, it being Family Day and all. Wonder if she wishes he'd walk in and surprise her. If he had a mind to walk back into our lives, this moment would be prime, 'cause he'd see Ma getting along without him, doing just fine, looking prettier than she ever did when he was around, and he'd want in on all this good stuff. Maybe he'd get down on one knee and propose again and beg to come back and take a stab at a fresh start. Fairy-tale wishing is as stubborn as a wart that won't die. And from the way Ma's smiling and talking to folks and getting along and setting up more cupcakes and punch, it looks like Daddy ain't even the crumb of her thoughts.

I help myself to another cup of punch, looking for anyone who might be in need of a granddaughter.

thirty-three

Once an idea, or a vision, as she calls it, grips the imagination of one Sydney Stevenson, she is all in, obsessively all in. Even if that idea wasn't originally hers, she will grab it like it's her baby doll and blast off, making all her dreams come true by bossing everyone about what to do. Put up posters! Pass out flyers! Sell tickets! She's talking to parents, talking with the pound, talking to teachers about decorations, advertising, getting word out to local news channels, music, food, drinks, bake sale, donations. . . . She got Pizza Oven to donate pizzas. She got PetSmart to donate chew toys. She got Party Plaza to donate balloons. She got a parent to build a dog-house photo booth.

Honest to angels, cross my heart, hope to die, I do not mind—not even a little itty-bitty bit—that someone other than myself, especially Sydney, is in the spotlight. Ain't that weird? It's like, who gives a flying fart?

I'm just feeling real good about what matters most: The Winter Rescue Dance is full-force on.

It's like the cafeteria is getting a makeover for tonight's dance. Larry puts up streamers with Nawsia. Sydney's on the hunt for the disco ball. Tables get covered with sheets of white plastic. Signs get painted on long sheets of butcher paper. Framed pictures of dogs and cats up for adoptions are used for centerpieces. Even Asa and his guys help by blowing up balloons. But once they start singing like Alvin and the Chipmunks, putting more helium in them than in the balloons, everyone swarms over to the tank so they, too, can sound like Alvin, Simon, and Theodore.

Sunny and I sit on the stage steps, cutting paw prints out of construction paper. For a dollar, you can buy a paw print, write your name on it, and tape it to the wall, goal being a wall of paws for a good cause.

"Those are some nice paws you're cutting," I tell Sunny.

"Yours don't look too nice. That look like baseball mitt," she says.

"Well, thanks a lot."

"Well, you welcome a lot."

What I really want to tell Sunny is that I missed her and it's nice to be cutting out paws together and I wish we could be best friends again and how's Howl-may doing, remember how she called me an angel, remember that? But instead I ask, "How'd you do yours?"

Sunny gives me one of her paw cutouts and says, "Here, you trace like this."

"Oh, duh. Why didn't I think of that?" I say, tracing her paw.

"Are you so excite about dance?" she asks.

"I can't wait. It's going to be a blast."

"You slow dancing with Larry?"

"Maybe. Since I told him to stop stalking me, he's been leaving me alone. I guess if I feel like slow dancing with him, I'm going to have to do the asking. Who do you want to dance with?"

She lowers her head while looking up through her bangs over to the balloon station.

"Asa?" I ask.

She bites down on her pinkie and nods, smiling sly and shy.

"Oh my Lordy, girl, I never would've guessed in a bazillion. You like Asa?"

She shakes her legs and flaps her hands like she's swatting mosquitoes and whines, "Don't say to nobody."

"Mum," I say, zip my lips, turn the key, and throw it across the cafeteria.

"I think I'm in the love," she says.

"Real?" I ask.

"He say hi to me. He call me Sunny J. That's so cool. He's so cool, right?"

"Man, you like him 'cause he said hi to you and called you a cool nickname? I thought you were smarter," I say.

"No. I am soooo dumb-dumb with the love," she says.

I laugh so hard I cut right through a paw.

She leans into me and whispers, "I don't know the slow dance. Do you know the slow dance? Did you do before?"

"I've danced with a boy, but it wasn't slow. So I guess to answer your question, no, I have not slow danced before, but how hard can it be? You just kind of sway, you know, left, right, left, right, kind of like a grandma on a sideways rocking chair. You have to face each other, but don't look at each other 'cause that's just too goo-goo-gah-gah, so you gotta look way over yonder and look like you're bored to death. His hands go on your waist and you put yours on his shoulders like a pair of shoulder pads. Right? Ain't that it? And then you rock to beat of the song. You'll feel it. And you have to hold your breath the whole time until one of you passes out. And whoever doesn't pass out wins," I say.

"Like this?" she says, and holds her breath, making a blow-up fish face.

"More like this," I say, and make a bigger blow-up fish face.

"Hey, Mickey, this is best dance idea," she says.

"I think so too."

"This your idea. Are you mad?"

"I'm not. Not even a little bit. I can't even try to feel mad. Ain't that something?"

"But no one say, 'Good job, Mickey,' and 'Mickey is so great to have great idea.' No one say that to you. Everyone say to Sydney."

"It's weird, right? You'd think I'd be all up in arms about not getting credit and recognition since I love me a spotlight, but it's like that part don't matter to me. What matters is those poor animals getting a chance."

"You change."

"You changed too."

"We suppose to change."

"I guess so."

"Is growing up."

"Are you still mad at me?"

"I was, but not now. Are you mad at me?"

"I was, but not anymore. Why'd we fight again?"

"I don't know. I think is my problem too. Sometimes, I feel like, ummmmm, you know like, ummmm . . . ," Sunny says, letting the scissors fall off her fingers onto her lap.

"Like what?"

"Like pet for Mickey."

"So you felt like my pet?"

"Yes. So I follow you too much. Because you so, you know, like, confident and so self-sure and talk loud and so friendly and you talk your mind just like that and you know English so good and you know America so good and I have bad English and I don't know and follow you like little pet. Sometimes I like, but sometimes I hate, and I want to go away from you and tell you, 'No, don't do like that.' Because the real friend is equal. Right? I want equal. Not like pet. Come here. Go there. Come over here. Do this. You mine. Good doggy. It bother me because it make me feel like a nothing, but I like you, but it bother me. So when Sydney like me, I don't want to go to her first time, but you say go, go, and I see I can go away. But Sydney the worst and treat like pet because my English is broke and she make so much teasing and squeeze my cheeks and call me Joo Joo, and I want to punch like this," she says, pumping her fists.

"Well, dang. First of all, that there looks more like cheering than fighting. And second of all, you are one deep dish," I say.

"So I do like this. Bam. Bam," she says, throwing punches into her palm.

"Yeah, that's tough."

"Yeah, tough and deep, but not like dish. I am deep like ocean. Let me asking, Mickey. Why you all need me to be like the pet?"

"I don't know. I didn't even know I was doing that. Like when? When did I treat you like my pet, 'cause I don't feel like I did. Give me, like, an example."

"You bossing me too much. You take like this and pull. Come here. Come here. Like this," she says, grabbing my wrist and tugging.

"Oh yeah. I did that, didn't I?"

"Like dog."

"I see it."

"And then you tell me wear this, wear that. Wear *hanbok*. I hate the *hanbok*."

"Then why'd you wear it? You didn't have to wear it."

"I know. So I say that my problem too. I have to fix. But making me so mad when you bossing me. Say like this. Say like that. You don't know. You no clue. You no clue," she says, imitating how I talk.

"Yeah, I get it."

"Just because my English not too good and I don't know how to do the American, it's not mean I'm dumb-dumb."

"Okay, for the record, I do not think you're a dumb-dumb. You are, like, wild smart. And, like, coming to this country and all and not speaking the language and doing what you're doing? That takes pure guts. And I think you deserve a standing O for that. That's how high I think of you. And I swear I did not mean to treat you like a pet, but I realize what I mean and don't mean don't matter 'cause you felt it, and I am from the bottom of my heart of hearts so sorry about all my bossing and tugging and telling you what to do and how to be like I'm some life pro, 'cause yeah, that would piss me off too. You're right. I didn't treat you equal. I guess it was 'cause I'm American, I thought I was some kind of expert and I took it upon myself to show you the ropes, you know, like a tour guide."

"Tour guide is not friend."

"I admit there was something about you being all lost and helpless like that that made me feel good about myself. I admit that. But then you were going off without me, being all powerful and doing your own thing, and I was like, 'Who does she think she is? I was her friend first. I found her. I made her. She's supposed to be mine.' Yeah, I get it. That was wrong. But you didn't have to spit your gum at me."

"No. I not spitting. I wrap and give to you like birthday present," she says, and laughs.

"That was nasty."

"So sorry, Mickey," she says, rubbing her hands.

Larry comes over to us, pinching a balloon, and squeaks, "Hey, what's up? Want to dance with me? How about we do the tango?"

Sunny and I would've laughed and thrown some

paws at him to go squeak somewhere else, if not for the scream. It was the scream to shut down all screams. Like Jason-is-chasing-me kind of scream. Like snakes-oozing-out-my-showerhead kind of scream.

From the other end of the cafeteria, Sydney bolts out of the kitchen, and she is screaming her head off and flailing her arms like streamers on a pom-pom. I've heard her scream plenty at rallies. This ain't no pep-rally scream.

A black cloud chases her out the kitchen. Like falling dominoes, everyone else starts screaming and scrambling and running for their lives out the doors.

The black cloud hasn't reached us on the stage yet, but Larry and Sunny go running off. I'm moving too, but I want to get a good look at this thing streaming out of the kitchen and spreading all over like—no, not like smoke; it's more like a bunch of flies. Flies. This here is an infestation of flies. I scream, flail my arms, and dash for the door 'cause I hate flies. One or two don't bother me none, but an entire generation makes me queasy sick like when Benny left a jar of jelly out and flies laid eggs in it that hatched into a bunch of flies crawling and swarming all over the jelly, and now I'm wondering if some of that stuff I took for raisins in all them school lunches I ate up were dead flies. The queasies hit me hard. I charge outside, only to run into Asa throwing up in the parking lot and Nawsia gagging and copy-cat retches sounding out like a chorus. I find me a spot behind the school sign and throw it all up.

I wipe my mouth and catch my breath, leaning against the signpost, which says SAVE LIVES. WINTER RESCUE DANCE TONIGHT. My queasies get taken over by the blues, 'cause it looks the dance can't happen with a bazillion flies infesting the cafeteria unless everyone's got a fly swatter and swats while dancing and don't mind that dead flies are floating in the punch. My queasies return. Looks like we're the ones in bad need of a rescue.

thirty-four

We're parked in front of the TV. Benny, Ma, Cyclops, Charlie, Jill, and even Kelly, who don't normally care to sprawl with us, sits on my lap. I guess she got a whiff of all the anticipation. We wait for the local news to come on. Reporter Pete Collins was at our school today. You know the type. He goes all out with the theatrics and loves pausing between his words for drama. He's. The. Best. His stories make me laugh, *tsk-tsk*, tear up, and want to get up and right all the wrongs in my neighborhood.

"Why's he look like a alien?" Benny asks, getting in front of the TV.

"Sit, Benny! I can't see. He's not an alien. He's a fly. That's a fly costume he's wearing," I say.

"Looks like a alien."

"Hush."

Pete Collins reports, "This is a story about the students of Landover Hills Middle School trying to save lives. The plan was to hold a dance tonight right here in their own cafeteria. Not just an ordinary dance. This dance was special. The dance of life or death. This dance would save lives. How?"

The camera cuts to Sydney. Oh my tarnation, that's Sydney, and the mic is on her, and she's talking to Pete Collins. "Our school partnered with the Prince George's County Animal Shelter. We were going to have this dance to raise money and awareness and basically give the cats and dogs that are, like, the most vulnerable a chance to get adopted, because if they don't get adopted, you know, it's really sad because, well, you know."

The camera cuts to a meowing tabby at the shelter. Then to a brown Lab in a crate curled into a doughnut. Then to a gray kitten pouncing and playing with a stuffed pig.

"Awwww," Ma, Benny, and I say in unison.

Oh my tarnation, that's Charity! Charity's on TV, and she's talking. "Winter's the worst for these animals. Our pound is packed. It's an emergency situation right now. We can't shelter every one of them. Believe me, we'd like to, but we just can't. There's no room. We have more animals coming in than going out."

"Then what happens to them?" Pete asks.

"Well, it's sad, but we have to, you know, put them down," Charity says.

"Put. Them. Down," Pete says, taking his dramatic pauses. "In other words, kill them. Euthanasia."

On the verge of tears, Charity nods.

"Why they kill kids in Asia?" Benny asks.

"Not youth in Asia. Euthanasia. It's mercy killing, which is a big fat lie, 'cause there ain't nothing merciful about it," I say.

The camera returns to Pete, who says, "These young people wanted to make a difference. They planned a school dance to find homes for abandoned cats and dogs who were on death row. They wanted to raise money to buy crates and toys for the shelter and save lives, but it's not going to happen, folks. The dance has been called off. Why? Why? Flies. You heard me. Flies."

Pete walks into our cafeteria. It's a mess. It looks like the apocalypse hit. The balloons have floated up to the ceiling. The streamers hang so sad and limp like toilet paper. Signs have fallen off the walls. It's embarrassing.

Pete moves into the school kitchen, saying, "While the students were decorating for the dance, they were attacked. Attacked by flies. Not a few flies, but a full-blown infestation not unlike a scene out of the Old Testament."

Oh my tarnation! That's Jamie. Jamie's on TV. He says, "It was pretty scary. This black cloud thing was like chasing everyone. There was all this screaming. Like, the girls were going crazy. I screamed too. We all ran."

Larry comes on and says, "It was like a scene from a horror movie."

Tammy says, "It was so gross."

Pete Collins comes back and says, "Gross, indeed. But it gets even grosser. The grossest. And according to the exterminator, it all started right here in the school kitchen."

The exterminator comes on and says, "We found some dead mice kind of throughout the place, but the real source was the grease trap. A lot of eggs got laid and hatched because of dead mice in there. That's what happens when the conditions are ripe. It's like the perfect storm for breeding flies."

Principal Farmer comes on and says, "It's awful. I feel for these kids. It's not just about the dance, but some of our students count on these meals, and we can't provide them until inspection gives us the go-ahead. You're talking two or three days to up to a week maybe."

"No lunch? What're we supposed to eat?" I say.

It's Mr. Graves. He says, "We're doing everything we can. We understand the urgency of the situation. Pest control got to the source of the infestation, and hopefully cleanup will be quick, and we'll pass inspection and get back to taking care of our students, our number-one priority."

"Mickey, why ain't you on?" Benny asks.

"I don't know. Maybe they cut that part. Hush. Pete's on," I say.

"This is a story of a chain of command flipped topsy-turvy. Aren't we, the people, supposed to be at the top of this chain? Then next rung down, it's our pets, the cats and dogs, and the cats chase the mice, and the mice eat the flies. Well, not in this case, folks. These flies took over, shutting down a school dance that would have saved the lives of some dogs and cats, who in turn would have helped control the mouse population, who in turn would have kept the flies in check. Flies won this battle, but will they win the war?"

"That's Mickey! That's Mickey!" Benny yells.

There I am. There's Sunny. There's Jack. There's Nawsia. I see Asa, too. We chase Pete Collins out of the cafeteria with fly swatters.

While we swat at him outside, he huddles over and says, "Pete Collins reporting. From Landover Hills Middle. Swatting out."

"I want to swat the alien. I want to get on TV. Mickey, you famous," Benny says.

"I wish," I say, petting Cyclops.

A commercial comes on. A man working under the

hood of a car looks up and complains about his head-
ache, saying how much he wants it gone. A woman
reading a book takes off her glasses, rubs her eyes, and
says her head throbs all over. A grandma petting her
dog suddenly stops and frowns, rubs her temples, and
says, "I don't have time for headaches." They take Advil,
the advanced medicine for pain, and like magic they're
back to living their lives. The man shuts the hood of the
car, smiling. The woman turns a page in her book, smiling. The grandma walks her dog, smiling.

"Ma?" I say.

"Mick?"

"I got an idea."

thirty-five

I t was what Ms. T would call a chain reaction. I talked to Ma. Ma talked to Jerry. Ma talked to Principal Farmer. Principal Farmer talked to Mr. Graves. Mr. Graves talked to the president of the PTA. The PTA president talked to the PTA board. I called Sydney. Sydney called the SGA kids. The SGA went through the school directory, and blast off! The rocket ship of telephone tag launched to reach every single student in our school.

Thanks to Pete Collins, we were all feeling it, the fire to stand up, right a wrong, do something, take action, rise, make it happen, work together, don't give up. The. Dance. Must. Go. On.

And the next thing you know, here I am, pouring myself a cup of the world's best punch at the Golden Gardens ballroom, watching an old woman in a wheelchair petting the cutest little cat on her lap, with Charity standing by. Halima and her parents check out a scrappy brown dog chasing its tail. Jermaine and his dad check out the most beautiful yellow Lab, but it's not as good-looking as Charlie. An old man sits at a table petting a dog that sits next to him like they belong together. He talks to the dog, and the dog wags its tail. Herman's got a kitten climbing his shoulder. Another woman gives treats to the most darling little poodle mix named Chelsea Ray. Most of the animals look all right with being here, except for the two dogs, huddled and hiding in the back corner, a chow and a husky. Benny sits with them, but they're shaking. Charity said the owner surrendered them yesterday, and they're scared and confused and attached to each other. Charity's also telling everyone being a foster family is a great way to provide temporary homes for these animals. Everyone's oooo-hing and awwwwing and what-do-we-have-here–ing, being real sweet and gentle 'cause animals got a way of bringing out the soft in us.

You'd think I'd be flying high happy we're pulling this miracle off, and a good chunk of me is, but another chunk of me—I guess you can call it the grumpy chunk—don't get how people up and leave their pets. You can tell yourself a buffet of bull-poop excuses about how life is so hard and this ain't what you bargained for and you got your own personal dreams to chase and the road owns you and you ain't getting any younger and how're you supposed to take care of yourself, let alone a wife, two kids, a dog, and three cats? So you split. It ain't fair. It's downright irresponsible. I spit at your splitting. But I refuse to waste my time and my happiness mulling and whining and boiling over about it. Life is good. Look at them beauties over there. Not one is hard. Not one is closed for business of getting and giving love. I want to be like that.

Sydney takes the leash of Chelsea Ray. She *would* pick the poodle mix. She stands at the doors with the dog, greeting everyone and passing out flyers about fostering and adopting. She's all smiles, welcoming students, their families, as well as the residents, while keeping an eye out for the news van. She's wearing the smartest-looking pantsuit. I swear, she's going to run the country someday.

Ma's at the dance floor, talking to the deejay, probably telling him to keep it oldies and easy listening on account of the residents. Without her, the Winter Rescue Dance at Golden Gardens would not be happening. I'm still in kind of a shock she took to my idea. It's more Pete Collins's doing than mine. We all got fired up. If we didn't get on TV, Ma would've said what she usually says when I tell her I got an idea. "In your dreams."

While Tony Bennett sings how the best is yet to come, Mr. Graves dances the fox-trot with his date. You heard me. He brought a date. Not in a bazillion would I have pegged him for a dancer, but I admit, he's pulling some smooth moves. Kids start to drag themselves to the dance floor like that's the last place they want to go, but oh all right, fine. Kevin dances with Joanna, which doesn't surprise me 'cause there's been talk about Joanna liking Kevin. Mike and Tracy start dancing together, and I'm like what's going on there 'cause they just broke up. Gina and Audrey partner up. Two girls dancing together is no big deal, so I don't get why two boys can't. They're all doing the hands-on-hips-and-shoulders, arms-stretched-forward zombie pose, eyes looking far and yonder, swaying to how we ain't seen nothing yet.

Principal Farmer goes table to table, shaking hands with parents, saying hi and thank you for supporting the students and reassuring everyone that the fly situation is under control.

Sunny walks in. I jump and wave. She jumps, waves back, and catwalks like a supermodel to the punch table. She's got on a black miniskirt, black knee-highs that look like boots from far away, a black turtleneck, and red lipstick. She's all these-boots-were-made-for-walking beatnik chic. I get her cup ready, pouring her some lime-green goodness topped with not one, but two maraschino cherries.

"Okay, you win the coolest cat," I say, handing her a cup of punch. "Here. Try this. It's so yummy."

She takes a sip and says, "Oh, so sweet. Is like the candy water."

"You got a foam mustache."

She licks it off and asks, "Is gone?"

"Yeah. Oh my tarnation, are those doggy earrings you're wearing? I love them. That's so cute. Your ears are pierced? When'd that happen? I gotta get mine pierced. Did it hurt?"

"It's like pinching."

"You know you can do it yourself with a needle and a ice cube and some rubbing alcohol. Hey, how'd you like my dress?" I ask, turning around.

"I like. I like. So cool. How did you make?"

"So easy-peasy. It's just cutting and stapling. I used duct tape to hold up the hem. See? It's just like a sack. Wear a big belt around it and voilà. This here's what I call the dress of the future. Hey, did you see Asa? He got on a tux," I say.

"I see. He look like penguin or something," Sunny says.

"What? I thought you were all goo-goo for him."

"I don't know if I like anymore. Too many girls like. I don't like that. Look at him. All those girls following around like that. I don't want."

"Honestly? I don't get what the big whoop is."

"I get. I think he's like celebrity. You know, like everybody know him. He's like star. That's why they like so much. Oh, Mickey, here come Larry."

"How do I look?" I ask, wondering why I even give two toots about how I look to Lawrence Elwood. Before Sunny can respond, I say, "Whatever. I don't care."

"He looking nice, Mickey," she whispers.

"Hey, what's up?" Larry says, getting some punch.

"Oh, hey," I say.

"Is it okay if I hang here with you guys?" he asks.

"Free country. It's fine by me," I say.

"Thanks," he says.

"You're welcome," I say, and sip my punch. I sip some more 'cause it feels like I should be the one doing the talking, but there ain't no words coming out of my mouth, which is weird, so the three of us stand in a quiet and awkward triangle, drinking a bunch of punch.

"This is really good punch," Larry says.

"Yeah, it's great punch. It's the ice cream. Lime sherbet? The lime-sherbet ice cream is what makes the punch so great. Sunny here thinks it's too sweet, but that's just her. I don't think anything can taste too sweet, if you ask me," I say, trying to drown the butterflies in my stomach with more punch. I don't know why I'm so nervous. I need to pee.

"I want to make the toast," Sunny says, holding up her cup.

"Yes, what a great idea! You go right ahead. Yes, please. Make a toast," I say, holding up my cup next to hers. Larry does the same. He looks at me and smiles. I think I smile back, but I can't tell 'cause my face feels asphalt-in-August hot. I don't know if it's the lighting in this room or what, but Larry looks cute. He combed his hair. Not a wrinkle in his blue shirt. Looks crispy, like a sheet of new paper. And he's wearing a skinny black leather tie. Throw me back, why don't you. His mouth looks like a mini hot dog bun. He smells all fresh, like a brand-new bar of Irish Spring soap.

"To our friend Mickey. She is the best friend," Sunny says.

I start to tear up. A lump forms in my throat.

"She calls me Sunny, but she is the one bringing all the sunshine, caring for the people and the animals who need friend the most and making everybody 'happy when the sky is gray,'" Sunny says, smiling so big her eyes crinkle. Then she sings, "'Please don't take my sunshine away,'" and taps our cups.

"To girls like you, Mickey," Larry says, tapping my cup.

"Stop. Y'all making me choke up. I'll have you know I ain't wearing waterproof mascara. Y'all going to make me look like Tammy Faye," I say, wiping my eyes and hugging Sunny.

She hugs me back, whispering into my ear, "Ask him to dance."

"You're so bossy," I whisper back.

The room dims. The disco ball comes on and spins, spotting the walls with moving lights. It's the Bee Gees. They start singing how they know my eyes in the morning sun and how we touch in the pouring rain, and my body moves automatic like one of them hula dolls on a dashboard. It's doing its own thing, and just like that, I ask Larry if he wants to dance with me, and the next thing you know, me and him, we're making our way to the dance floor together to the sound of Sunny's silly applauding behind us, and I'm trying to look like I've done this, like, a thousand times, it's nothing, just like breathing, but sweat puddles in my pits and a bead trickles down my arm and a salty mustache forms on my upper lip and I still need to pee. Larry puts his hands on my waist. A staple pricks and tickles my side. I wiggle and laugh, which makes Larry's face drop into a what-did-I-do-wrong look? I move his hands up a little and say, "Staples." He nods, *oh okay*, like he knows what I'm talking about. I tell him I got staples holding my dress together and place my hands on his shoulders and rock left right, left right to the Bee Gees asking how deep my love is, but I can't get into it 'cause this feels like how Frankenstein would dance. And I ain't no Frankenstein.

Then Larry starts to sing, which cracks me up. First of all, I can't believe he knows the words. Second of all, he can't sing, and he knows he can't, but he don't care, and he's making those desperate faces like he's singing his heart out. I laugh. I also relax enough to shut off my sweat fountain and stop doing the Frankenstein. I hold his hands instead and just move along to the song. Then I let go and move like I do in my own living room. Larry's doing his own thing, snapping his fingers, and every once in a while he twirls me and I twirl him back. It's so much fun I don't want it to end.

But it does 'cause the deejay plays "It's Electric."

When the Electric Slide comes on, the dance floor gets swarmed. Everyone—I mean everyone—kids and teachers and parents and all the old folks, don't matter if you got a wheelchair or cane or a walker or two left feet. Everyone dances the Electric Slide.

Benny even pops out of nowhere and dances his own take next to me and Sunny. Never mind he moves like a windup toy. Sydney puts down her flyers to join in. Of course, Tammy and Nawsia follow her. Mr. Graves works up a sweat. Principal Farmer's arms are up in the air, circling like a pair of lassos. Some old woman's bracelets jangle like tambourines. Asa's making his own moves in the front corner, popping and locking. Herman looks like he's hardly moving, but he's moving all right 'cause his toupee wiggles.

While we dance, I notice some girls sitting around that old woman with the fancy clothes and big bracelets. She's telling them something. I have no idea what she's saying, but she's got their undivided attention. Then the girls burst out laughing.

Everyone's having such a time. This is the closest I've come to feeling high on the hog. I wish we could do this again. And as soon as I see Ma standing at the door talking to her boss, I get an idea.

thirty-six

Ok sent me a drawing of Cyclops poking her head out of a tent with a bubble that says, "Thanks, Mickey. You saved meow life."

Hey Ok,

Thanks for the picture. I'd draw something for you, too, but I got too many words in me that need to come out. You ever feel like that? I never thought I was any good at writing. I'm good at talking, I know that, but I was always getting Cs and Ds in language arts class, so I steered clear of reading and writing, but I like writing you. It feels different. It sits right. It's not fake like the school stuff. When I write you, I can hear my inner voice.

Anyway, long story short, we had this miracle school dance that helped get foster care for 3 cats and 4 dogs and forever homes for 2 cats and 3 dogs. Not bad, huh? Do the math. That's a dozen lives saved. It was a miracle 'cause it wasn't supposed to happen on account of the school cafeteria getting infested with dead mice and flies. Gross. I know. Did you see me on TV? We ended up holding the dance at Ma's work. Which was a total blast. We all had so much fun. By "all," I mean old folks, young folks, parent folks, and animal folks. And don't get all jealous, but I even slow danced for the first time with a boy. Do you remember Lawrence Elwood? Everyone calls him Larry now. I think he's got a crush on me. Well, we slow danced together. AWKWARD. I was sweating like a faucet.

Anyway, while we were all dancing, I had this idea. It struck me so strong. What if our school partnered with Golden Gardens? What if we had an after-school program that let the students and seniors hang out? Like tell stories, play cards, do homework . . . you know, chew the fat. I know a lot of these old folks are plain bored and lonely and feeling useless. A bunch of us kids feel the same way. I told Ma about it. She's going to talk to her boss and Principal Farmer.

Anyway, want to hear something weird? I think I'm getting to be more like you, Ok. A nerd.

I'm getting As and Bs this year. Honor roll. Not one C or D. Coming from me, that's, like, a miracle. If I keep this up, I might be well on my way to college. I'll be the first in my family. Unless my supermodeling career takes off. Ha-ha. But seriously, never in my 13 years would I have guessed that the year Daddy don't come back is the year I'd do my best in school. What's up with that?

Writing you's mooding me into some deep thoughts. Get your floaties on 'cause I'm diving into the deep end. What does it mean to succeed? Is it getting good grades? Is it getting money? Is it being popular? Is it having fun? Is it having friends? Is it getting applause? Is it about being strong? Is it about helping people? Is it about helping yourself? I don't know. I think it's a mix of all those things.

One thing I do know for sure is that it's about getting back up and not staying down when you do fall. And everyone falls down. Speaking of falling, I gave my roller skates away. They got way too small for me, so I gave them to this girl who lives in our building. Her name's Leyla, and she always looked like she was bored out of her mind, so I gave them to her. I saw Leyla rolling around in them, falling and getting back up and figuring it all out, and that made me feel really happy. Like some crack in my heart was getting filled up with the glue of gold.

Do you know about this glue of gold thing they used way back when to mend broken bowls? Sunny told me all about it. She said that there used to be this old way of mending broken bowls with this special glue that was made of gold to put all the pieces back together again. The glue was gold, so it was like you were showing off the cracks instead of trying to hide them. Isn't that something? The bowl didn't look the same as before 'cause it had all this gold running through it like roads on a map. The bowl ended up being stronger and more beautiful and more valuable than before it was broke. I've been thinking a lot about this.

It's kind of like we're all bowls. We get made. We get used. We get dropped. We break. And I guess we can stay broke, but I believe in my heart of hearts we all got the glue of gold running through us and we can help bring one another's broken pieces back together again, and we end up being better, more beautiful and stronger than ever. That's what life means to me. That's what success means to me. I guess it's nice not to never

ever break, but what's the fun in that? I don't know about you, but I want to be made of trails and rivers and roads of gold holding me together, but that's just me being me.

Always here,
Mickey

thirty-seven

You should keep your shoes on unless you want furry feet like mine," I say to Sunny as she squats to untie her sneakers. I show her my wiggling socks, which look like a pair of newborn pups.

"I like the furry feet," she says, taking her shoes off. Sunny smells springtime fresh, like a Saturday afternoon in April.

Charlie's wagging tail makes so much wind, it's like he's got a fan on his butt. I tell him to sit. He sits. Sunny pets him and says, "Good dog. Good dog. So big." Charlie rolls onto his back, inviting belly scratches. Sunny laughs. I scratch his belly and tell him to scram.

Benny comes running out to the living room in his underwear, announcing to the whole wide world that he did a clogger.

"I need you . . . ," he starts to say, and slows down, noticing Sunny standing in our apartment staring at him. "To plunge," he finishes, staring back at her.

"Who're you?" he asks.

"I'm Sunny. Hi, Benny," she says.

"How do you know me?"

"From the dance. Nice to see you again," she says, putting out her hand to shake his.

"I wouldn't do that. He just pooped," I tell her. She puts her hand away.

"You here to play?"

"Yeah, just hanging out."

"Well, toilet's clogged," he says, and runs back.

"Wash your hands and put on some clothes," I yell after him.

"Ma said take a bath."

"Fine, then take a bath."

"That's what I was going to do, but the toilet clogged. You have to plunge or it's going to flood like last time."

"Fine!"

I turn to Sunny and say, "Hey, you like pancakes?"

"I love pancake."

"Want to make some with me?"

"Yes! Let's make it!"

We go to the kitchen. I get out everything we need: pancake mix, oil, frying pan, bowl, spatula, and fork. I pour some mix into the bowl and water it at the faucet. Sunny pours oil into the frying pan and turns on the heat. I mix the batter, add more water, mix some more until it's just right.

"Thank you for having me to come over, Mickey. This is so fun."

"I know. I been wanting to have you over for, like, ever—ever since you had me over your place for chew-suck. Did I say that right? Chew-suck? Don't it feel like that was like a million years ago but at the same time it feels like it was just yesterday?" I say, spooning mix into the hot oil. It spreads into a perfect circle. The edges sizzle.

"Where your mom go?" Sunny asks.

"She works on the weekends."

"Where your dad go?"

"Heck if I know. He don't live with us. They're getting a divorce," I say, flipping a pancake.

"I'm so sorry, Mickey. That's too sad."

"It's all right. I'm all used to it now. I've actually been doing better than when I used to wait around like a dummy for him to come home, and he never stayed long anyway. The waiting was a total waste. And I'll have you know that this is my best year yet in school. I got more friends. I'm getting more stuff done. I got better grades. Can you believe that? I ain't getting a single D this year. That's, like, a miracle. And lo and behold, I think I'm even getting an A in science on account of you being my lab partner. I done fine without him. Sometimes I think he might could've been the thorn in my side. He missed out on so much. The big stuff like birthdays and holidays, yeah. But he missed out on the everyday boring stuff too. That's the stuff a life's built on. All in all, I think I'm stronger for it. That's how I see it. What don't kill you makes you stronger. That's my motto," I say.

"Oh, Mickey."

"Don't get me wrong. Oh man, what I would do for my day in court. I'm not waiting around for it or anything, but I want me some answers. I see it like this. Like he's sitting in that box, can't go driving off nowhere, and I'm walking around the courtroom and asking him questions like them lawyers do. I even got on a suit and tie."

"What you asking?"

"All sorts of stuff. But I guess what my heart of hearts really wants to know is why. Like why? Why don't he want us? Why don't he want me? I don't get that part. I'm great. I'm smart. I'm fun. I'm kind. Heck, look at me. I'm a beauty. I get stuff done. I cook some mean pancakes. I care. I'm not perfect, but I'm good. I'm really good. I know I am. So why don't he want me?" I ask, looking down at the pancakes. My eyes well up with tears, and my mouth starts quivering into a crybaby face. Sunny looks up at me. The pancakes sizzle.

She hugs me tight and says, "Oh, Mickey, I don't

know. I never meet your father, but I think he is very lost and sad and stupid man, because you are the best."

We hug long enough for the edges of the pancakes to cook crispy brown. I wipe my tears. Sunny wipes her tears too. We plate the first batch.

"Hey, Benny! Benny! If you want pancakes, come and get it now or they're all going to be gone!" I yell out.

I listen for him, but he don't answer. The bath water runs. He can't hear me.

"Great. No syrup. Figures," I say, shutting the fridge. "You have sugar?"

I open a cabinet. No sugar. I open another cabinet. No sugar, but we got a thing of SlimFast. "Hey, want to make chocolate pancakes?" I ask, opening it up.

"Okay, but not all. Let's make half chocolate," she says.

I open the junk drawer. Sugar packets. Mustard packets. Ketchup packets. "Syrup! We got syrup!" I yell.

"Yay!" she says, jumping up and down.

We finish frying up the pancakes, stack two towers on a plate, and squeeze the packets of syrup on top. It's not enough, so we use up the sugar packets and sprinkle those on too. It smells so good. We head outside to the balcony. I set the plate of pancakes on a milk crate, and we sit across from each other on the concrete floor. It's all dusty with pollen, but we don't care. We dig in.

"So good. We make it the best," Sunny says, giving me a thumbs-up.

"This is the best. Beats IHOP, don't it?" I say, cutting through seven layers of pancakes with the side of my fork.

The patio door slides open, and there stands Benny all cleaned up. His hair's combed down flat with a part to the side. He's wearing his dress pants and dress shirt. They're all wrinkly. He missed a button, so one side of the shirt hangs lower than the other. He looks like he's ready for church.

"Why you all dressed up?" I ask, but I know why. It's 'cause of Sunny.

He shrugs and says, "I want some."

"Come sit here, Benny," Sunny says, dusting pollen off the floor.

I give him a forkful of pancake and he eats it, chewing with his mouth closed. He's putting on his best manners for Sunny, and it's making me crack up inside, but I ain't going to say nothing.

The three of us sit around the crate, the pancakes disappearing fast. They taste so sweet and soft with a little crunch on the edges. I'd say they're the best I've had, and I've had my share.

Sunny says something about how nice Benny looks, and I swear he turns so pink it's like I'm sitting next to a slice of watermelon.

Cyclops comes walking out and climbs on my lap, nestling against my foot like I'm her favorite place in the world.

Yellow dandelions cover the patch of grass in front of our building. I used to pick those. I used to string them into necklaces and bracelets and rings, pretending I was a princess. Once I even strung together a great big mane, called myself Dandy the lion, roared until my throat got sore, and blew at all the fuzzy seed balls like they were birthday candles, doing all sorts of crazy wishing. Seeds floated all around me like pixie dust, landing who knows where.

thirty-eight

Never thought I'd see this day, but it's here. Took long enough. It's the last day of school. We are done done done!

I'm going over to Sunny's. We walk together from the bus stop, swinging our arms like a pair of kindergartners skipping up Sesame Street. We're all giggles. Anything and everything's making us laugh. Crack in the sidewalk. Crows cawing from the sky. Our growling stomachs. Clouds shaped like flying saucers.

It's hot for June.

We had an awards assembly today. I knew I was getting an honor roll certificate, which is a first for me, but what I didn't know was I got voted a superlative by my peers. They gave me Best Neighbor. Mr. Graves said it goes to the student who shows she cares about our community and the ones who tend to get forgotten. I got a lot of cheers for that. It's a memory I'm holding and tucking away for safekeeping.

Sunny got on the Principal's List, which means she got straight As. Isn't that nuts? First time in a new country, struggling to speak English, and she makes straight As.

Oh, and Sydney got Best Hair. Can't disagree with that. The girl's got good hair.

We walk through Sunny's door.

"Halmae, *dora wasseob nida*!" Sun Joo yells.

"What'd you say?" I ask.

"It's just like 'I'm back.' Say like this. *Dora*."

"*Dora*," I say.

"*Wasseob*," she says.

"*Wasseob*. That's like 'What's up,'" I say.

"No, not 'What's up.' *Wasseob*," she says.

"*Wasseob*," we say.

"*Nida*," she says.

"*Nida*," I say.

"*Dora wasseob nida*," we say together.

"That's not bad. That's good. So when you come back after you go out, then you say '*Dora wasseob nida*,' like, 'Hey, I'm back,'" Sunny says.

Howl-may's cooking some kind of soup on the stove. She opens the lid to show us the little fishies tumbling around in the bubbles. A big ball of dough is on the countertop. Her hands are powdered white with flour.

"Oh, yum!" I say.

Howl-may says something to Sunny. Then I follow her to her bedroom, where we drop off our backpacks and go to the bathroom to wash our hands. We squeeze in tight together in front of the sink, passing around the bar of soap, lathering up our hands until they're sudsy and slippery.

Howl-may gives each of us a ball of dough to knead, saying something in Korean.

"What she say?"

"She say to do like this and make soft and make into ball," Sunny says, kneading her piece. I copy her.

Sunny shows me her lump of dough. It's perfect like a Ping-Pong ball. I shape mine like hers. We watch Howl-may take a rolling pin and spread out her big dough ball flat and even and smooth.

"Looks like pizza. She ain't going to throw that up in the air, is she?" I ask.

"No. She going to cut into noodle. See? It's the knife noodle," Sunny says.

Howl-may folds the flat dough over five times so it looks like a rolled-up rug, then takes a knife and cuts it into strips until there's a hill of noodles.

"That's so neat. So that's how you make noodles. I always thought they came in a box," I say.

We do like Howl-may and roll our dough balls flat, fold them over, and cut them into strips. We add ours to her hill of noodles, and she takes the whole pile and drops it into the bubbling broth. Howl-may stirs the pot.

We wait. My mouth waters. No one's saying nothing 'cause we want noodles in our mouths now.

Howl-may turns around and looks at us waiting there and giggles. She tastes the broth, shakes some powder into it, and stirs. Finally, she fills the first bowl, then a second bowl. Two bowls of knife-noodle soup on a tray. She carries it out to the dining table, and like two hungry strays, we follow her. She sets each bowl down, and we take our seats and dig in, slurping up noodles, which are fat, meaty, bumpy, and chewy. I never had noodles like these. I never had broth like this either, but it tastes so snug it reminds me of home.

I start tearing up.

"What's matter?" Sunny asks.

"It's just so good," I say.

"This one my favorite," she says.

"Howl-may, *go map seum nida*," I say in my best Korean. It means "thank you."

Laughing and nodding, she says, "You way come."

I eat. You know how when something's so good you want to share it so bad? Like it's a shame not everyone's in on it? That's how this noodle soup makes me feel. It's so good. It tastes like comfort. Like someone's looking